Hunting Harker

When Ollie Harker's wagon fails to arrive at Logjam Creek, his employer, J.B. Cookson, hires Tom Parry and Durango Finch to find it. It appears that Harker has been killed by hostile Indians, but when a murder in the town is linked to him, Harker's mission is revealed to be something more than a routine freighting operation.

The trail leads Parry and Finch to an illegal whiskey-running operation in which Monson, Logjam Creek's saloon owner, is implicated. But getting proof of this is both difficult and dangerous, and the two hunters find themselves in deep peril when they come up against a ruthless gang of moonshiners.

Hunting Harker

Greg Mitchell

A Black Horse Western

ROBERT HALE

© Greg Mitchell 2017
First published in Great Britain 2017

ISBN 978-0-7198-2451-7

The Crowood Press
The Stable Block
Crowood Lane
Ramsbury
Marlborough
Wiltshire SN8 2HR

www.bhwesterns.com

Robert Hale is an imprint
of The Crowood Press

Typeset by
Derek Doyle & Associates, Shaw Heath
Printed and bound in Great Britain by
CPI Group (UK) Ltd, Croydon, CR0 4YY

ONE

It was the third day of the search for Ollie Harker when Tom Parry found the tracks that he suspected were caused by the missing man's wagon. His elation turned to apprehension however when, seconds later, he saw the carefully regulated puffs of white smoke rising against the clear blue sky. He had almost forgotten that his current job contained no small element of danger. Checking his strawberry roan horse, he stood in the stirrups and looked around before waving his hat to attract the attention of two approaching riders, who were followed by a pack mule.

One of the pair, a wiry little middle-aged man with a short grey beard, took his eyes from the smoke as though it was inconsequential, turned in the saddle and spoke to his companion:

'Looks like young Tom has found something.'

'I'm not wishing him any harm,' his companion replied, 'but if it's what's left of Ollie Harker I won't complain. I'm past the stage where I enjoy riding about where I might meet people who want to kill me.'

The speaker was in his late thirties, powerfully built, better dressed than his companions and sporting a pair of Smith & Wesson .44s with forward-pointing butts high on his hips. His face, with its drooping black moustache, was that of a man who seldom smiled. His clothes were new and almost clean, as were his highly polished expensive black boots. He sat in a silver-mounted saddle on a well-bred black horse. Hired guns made good money and Durango Finch was determined to enjoy life's luxuries while he lived. A realist by nature, he had serious doubts about reaching old age. He might not recognize the man who shot faster and straighter until it was too late.

'By the look of that smoke,' he told Joe Murchison, 'we might not have too many friends around here. I hope Parry's found something important.'

'Anything's better than nuthin',' the little man muttered. He set his bay mare cantering towards where Parry was waiting.

Finch watched the smoke for a second or two and sincerely hoped that the search was coming to an end. He did not share the eagerness of his two companions. If trouble was coming he would not shy away from it but he was in no hurry to be risking his life. With an air of resignation he turned his horse and followed Murchison. Parry was pointing ahead when the others arrived.

'I reckon those are the tracks of Harker's wagon. They're weeks old but wheels leave prints that stay for months. You can see where they went through that long grass over there. If we head in that direction we're sure to find more sign.'

'What if we find Indians instead?' Durango asked. His mind was still on the signal smoke. The tracks were harmless but his well-developed sense of self-preservation and his gut instinct told him there was danger in the smoke.

'That's where you start earning your money,' Murchison told him bluntly. He was not particularly sure that he liked Durango.

'J.B. Cookson seems to think you're a one-man army. If you're half as good as folks say a few Indians won't worry us.'

'Any man with a gun who might want to kill me sure worries me, Murchison. A lucky shot can kill you just as quick as a carefully aimed one. What if these tracks lead us into an ambush?'

'That's why Tom is here. He has to make sure that doesn't happen. Don't be fooled by his age, he's a good tracker; he knows this country and he knows Indians – and more than a few of their tricks.'

'That leaves you,' Durango said. 'What are you good at?'

Murchison glared briefly at the questioner before replying sharply to what he considered an impertinent question.

'I'm mighty good at looking after J.B.'s interests. I was his wagon master for twenty years and I know his likes and dislikes. He's built a big freight-hauling business but lately he's got a mite peeved since someone stole Harker's wagon and probably killed poor old Ollie at the same time.'

7

The gunfighter frowned. 'I still don't see what was so special that he couldn't leave this problem to the law or the army.'

'J.B. ain't like that. A lawman might come through here every six months or so but it's only for appearances' sake, and the army are tied up chasing hostile Indians. J.B. looks after his own. But this wagon wasn't carrying freight. It was bringing office records to that new base he is setting up at Logjam Creek. Can't see much sense in all that paper stuff myself but J.B. reckons you can't run a good business without it. He figures it's important and he wants it found nearly as much as he wants to find Harker.'

'I wouldn't be too hopeful about that paperwork.' Parry joined the conversation. 'Chances are some Cheyenne squaw is using Cookson's books to start fires. I reckon the most important thing is what happened to Harker. He's driven over the trails around here for years. He wouldn't get lost or take a wrong turn but these tracks are miles off the proper trail. From what we know of him he's hardly likely to steal a wagon and team, so it figures that something unusual has happened.'

'I can't understand why he didn't stay with the wagon train,' Durango said. 'Going off on your own when the Cheyenne are on the prod doesn't sound to me like a real smart idea.'

'He travelled most of the way with the other wagons,' Murchison explained, 'but they were headed for Oregon so he had to leave the main overland trail. He had a good mule team that was lightly loaded and

J.B. wanted the records as quick as possible. It was an easy two-day drive to Logjam Creek so he went alone. Most of our drivers have done the same thing with no problems. He was not to know that the Cheyennes were off the reservation.'

'Neither did I when I took this job,' Durango muttered ruefully. From his Civil War service to the present he had seen plenty of hot lead directed his way but he had never fought Indians. He was basically a townsman whose western battlefields had been mostly in saloons or town streets. He had survived because of his shooting ability, a cautious nature and a reluctance to go into fights where he did not know the odds against him.

'Do you reckon that signal smoke was about us?' he asked Parry.

'I don't rightly know. It is usually a signal arranged in advance. We might have been spotted but it could just be a sign to bring other war parties together. That's the worrying bit. It shows there are more than one bunch of troublesome Indians around here somewhere.'

Murchison growled. 'Don't worry too much about Indians. Just in case you might be thinking that we ought to turn back, we ain't getting paid to be spooked by the first sign of trouble. We go on until we find that wagon or the situation gets too dangerous. This ain't a suicide trip but we need to have something to tell J.B. If things get too serious we won't hang around. But I'll do the deciding about when we run.'

'Fair enough,' Durango agreed, although the tone

of his voice implied that his agreement could be conditional.

Parry made no comment but wondered if Durango might be starting to lose his nerve. He was a little surprised that a man of such a reputation should already be anxious about the task before them. The gunman had not previously shown anxiety about the prospect of an Indian fight. Now that it was a real possibility he appeared to be having second thoughts.

It was also possible that Durango might have unknowingly invited what could be serious trouble. Though he said nothing, Parry knew that the gunman's silver hatband and silver-mounted saddle were likely to glint in the bright sunlight and catch the eyes of Indian scouts. Such advertising made his own job harder but he was determined to do his part. Now he would take charge for a while.

'I'll go ahead and read the tracks,' he told the other two men. 'Follow about a hundred paces behind. But keep your eyes peeled. That open country looks flat but there are dips in the ground where you could hide a whole troop of cavalry – and those trees on the slopes over there could hide a mighty big war party.'

If the older men had any objections to his plan he did not hear them as he set spurs to the roan and cantered away. When he considered that he was the required distance in front he slowed his mount to its usual fast walk.

Ahead lay the long grassy plain but on their left, about half a mile away, was a range of cedar- and pine-covered hills. The hill from where they had seen the signal was a fair way off along the same range. Parry hoped that the signallers had not seen them on account of the distance but he was aware that this could be dangerous wishful thinking. Until it proved otherwise he would assume that their presence had been observed and that those who had made the smoke probably had unfriendly intentions.

The grassland gave way to a wide expanse of red soil partially covered by sagebrush and, as expected, the wheelmarks of the wagon showed plainly. The bare earth also revealed the hoofprints of horses on both sides of the wagon tracks. Again Parry halted and read the signs as he waited for the others. When they joined him, he told them what he had learned.

'Harker had company when he reached here. Looks like two riders on each side of the wagon – three unshod ponies, one shod American horse. Likely he could have been a prisoner or already dead. These characters probably ambushed him on the main trail and took him this way.'

'Are we looking for a white man and three Indians?' Murchison asked.

'I don't know. The shod horse could be a stolen one. It could be four Indians or it could be four white men. Lots of folks ride unshod ponies at times.'

'Either way it don't look too good for Harker,' Durango growled.

With a growing feeling of impending danger they continued at a brisk walk, sitting alert in their saddles and casting apprehensive glances around them. A few minutes later Parry rode over a slight rise. In a small hollow beyond it he found the burnt remains of a wagon. Mostly it was a mass of blackened, charred timber. If it had not been for rusted iron tyres, a few metal fittings and the odd unburnt scrap of canvas, the mass of ash and charcoal would have been unrecognizable.

'Looks like you found the wagon,' Durango said as he rode to where the tracker was waiting. 'The Cheyenne did a good job of destroying it.'

'Too good a job,' Parry murmured, half to himself. 'Looks like someone kept pushing the pieces together to make sure it was really destroyed. Why would Indians do that?'

Murchison pushed his big mare to the front.

'Wait here,' he ordered. 'I want a close look at this. Any papers will be well and truly gone but what's left of Ollie is probably around here somewhere – might even be under these ashes.'

The wagon master dismounted when he reached the charred wreckage. He studied it closely, occasionally stirring up little black clouds as he walked through the cold ashes. A short while later he stopped and peered at the ground.

'There's tracks here,' he called. 'See what you make of them, Tom.'

As he urged his horse forward Parry saw what appeared to be wagon tracks beyond where the fire had been. He urged his horse closer and, by force of habit, he also did another check of their surroundings. He shifted his gaze to the mountains on their left just in time to see the tiny figures of horsemen emerging from the trees on the lower slopes. They were riding in single file and appeared to be in no hurry. Even at a distance there was something menacing about the riders and he felt the hairs rise on the back of his neck.

'There's Indians coming,' he called to Murchison. 'Looks like trouble.'

'Trouble for them if they try anything,' the wagon master growled. He had picked up a stick and, with great concentration, was prodding it among the ashes. Durango slid his Remington rifle from its saddle scabbard and flicked up the rear aperture sight. Suddenly his nervousness was gone.

'Just say the word, Joe. I can pick off a couple when they come in to about three hundred yards. I won't try any further away; I like to be sure of my shots.'

'You'd best get on your horse, Joe,' Parry called, more urgently now. 'There's trouble heading this way. Those Indians are not paying us a social call.'

'I want more time to look around. Durango, see if you can hold them at long range. See what you make of these tracks, Tom.'

Parry rode to where he could see the tracks Murchison had discovered. Wind erosion had blurred the imprints of a white man's boots but traces remained among the partially obscured hoofmarks around the site. At least one white man had been present. But could the track be that of the missing driver? Parry was curious too about what looked like wagon tracks showing on a patch of bare earth ahead. Why had the raiders backed the wagon into the hollow before they burned it?

Durango called from his vantage point.

'Those Indians have stopped for some reason. They're not coming into range, just riding back and forth watching us. Do you want me to try a shot? I can shoot close enough to scare someone.'

'Just keep watching them but shoot if they come closer,' Murchison ordered. He turned to Parry but that man was no longer interested in tracks.

'Get on your horse, Joe,' the younger man said urgently. 'It's time we got out of here.'

'What do you mean? The Indians can't hurt us from that far away and there's only a handful of them. Durango is keeping a close eye on them.'

'That's what they want. While we are watching them you can bet that an ambush party has slipped past us into the trees over there. Those hostiles are just there to herd us into the trap. We have to go right now before they have a chance to get around us.'

'I dunno . . .' Murchison began, still not fully convinced.

'I do. We have to get out right now. Get on your goldarned horse. It's a trap.'

Frowning and doubtful, the wagon master mounted and reluctantly joined the others.

'They'll come out of the trees on our right when we make a run for it. They might be ahead of us or a bit behind us. We might have to shoot our way through them,' Parry explained. 'If you find yourself close to one with a bow, try to get on his right side. They don't miss too often with arrows but it is harder for an Indian to get a good shot at you when he's on a horse and you happen to be on his right. They like to chase on both sides – like they run buffalo. If their targets strike some obstacle ahead they have to turn to one side or another and that puts them closer to the hunters on that side.'

Durango returned his rifle to its saddle scabbard and drew a revolver. The others loosened their Colts in their holsters as they set spurs to their horses.

The watching braves set up a yell when they saw the white men galloping away. One fired a shot, more as a signal than an attempt to hit anyone. Then the pursuit began.

The pounding of their horses' hoofs drowned out the distant war cries but a quick backward glance showed that the hunters had surged after the fleeing trio. Parry had been expecting that. It was a known fact that Indians would pursue anyone who fled from them. Now in full flight, the riders had to concentrate on where they were riding.

The ground they had ridden over previously was safe enough at a slow pace but at high speed the rough terrain could easily bring down a horse. Small obstacles and broken ground suddenly became hazards and the riders' first priority was to steer the safest course. All of them remembered passing several prairie dog villages, which would bring down any horse that galloped into them. They had covered about half a mile when Durango shouted:

'There they are – over on the right, just coming out of the trees.' Checking his horse slightly, the gunman allowed the others to go ahead while he switched to the right side so that he would be closest to the hunters when both groups merged.

'Stay close together and only shoot at those who get in front of us,' he yelled. 'I'll take any on this side. Count your shots and don't waste any. You might not get a chance to reload.'

TWO

Parry had no time to count them but he estimated that about twenty warriors were riding hard to intercept them. He had never subscribed to the notion that one white man could whip half a dozen Indians and he dared not consider what could happen in the next minute or two. He had to push all doubts to the back of his mind and think clearly.

The rattle of hoofs behind him suddenly registered on his consciousness. Surely none of the Cheyennes could be that close behind him? Alarmed, he glanced back and saw Murchison's pack mule trying to keep up with them but his relief was short-lived because a quick sideways glance showed the war party converging at an angle that would bring about a collision between hunters and hunted.

A few warriors on the swiftest mounts had outrun their comrades. They yelled in triumph and brandished weapons as they guided their mounts closer. Urged on by rawhide quirts the Cheyennes' ponies, with necks stretched and bellies close to the ground, were rapidly closing the distance.

Parry and Murchison now drew their guns, alert for riders who might evade Durango and get in front of them.

The gunman himself let his horse choose its own path while he studied the foremost riders. The nearest one was fitting an arrow to a bow when Durango took his first shot. The warrior would be shooting to his left, so the gunman had to get him before he could release the arrow. Though hastily aimed, the bullet knocked the brave from his pony and the arrow went up into the air as it was involuntarily released by the stricken man. Almost casually Durango fired again and picked off the next rider, who had narrowly missed him with a shot from a Sharps carbine.

He missed his third shot as the Cheyenne dropped down on his pony's offside. The animal cut in front of Murchison's horse, causing it to shy violently. Almost unseated, the angry wagon master wasted a shot at the tiny amount of his body that the warrior showed.

Parry chose an easier target and shot the horse as the attacker crossed his path. He was not sure where his bullet struck but the animal went down in a cloud of dust and threshing legs. Almost without breaking stride the roan horse hurdled the fallen pony. Parry caught a momentary glimpse of an upturned painted face as the horse landed clear of the frantically rolling brave.

Durango's next shot sent another brave somersaulting backwards over his horse's rump. Four men had paid the price for leaving their comrades too far behind. He looked for his next target but the warriors had reined in their eager ponies. They halted in a milling bunch, shouting angrily and firing the odd futile shot at the rapidly retreating white men.

'We stopped 'em,' Durango shouted in obvious relief. 'They're not game to take us on. I didn't think they'd give up because of a few losses.'

'It's not a few losses to them,' Parry explained. 'They have a lot of trouble replacing braves who get killed. But don't start celebrating too soon. They know there are only three of us. I think they'll try again and next time they'll be a lot smarter.'

Murchison glanced back over his shoulder. 'They're still just milling about back there. When Indians have got the odds on their side, they don't give up this easy. I can't figure out why they stopped.'

'Thank your lucky stars they did, Joe. If you had delayed another half-minute we would have had to fight our way through the whole war party instead of just a couple of their fastest riders. Our scalps are more important than the ashes of Cookson's wagon.'

'I thought that Ollie Harker's body might have been there somewhere,' the wagon master replied sheepishly. Murchison was not a man who readily admitted his mistakes; somehow the words sounded unconvincing, as though Murchison was not being completely honest and was holding something back.

'They nearly had us,' Durango interrupted. 'I saw enough close-range mounted fights in the war to know that some of our horses would surely have been hit. Why do you think they stopped?'

Parry could only make an educated guess. 'Chances are that one of those braves that you shot was a war chief or even a medicine man. I expect they might talk things over for a while but they most likely will come after us again. Don't forget those smoke signals. They might just be waiting for more help to arrive. Let's reload our guns and let these horses catch their wind. We can't afford to run them to exhaustion.'

The mule caught up with them as they slowed their horses. It was unharmed but a couple of arrows were lodged in its pack. Murchison swore, waited for the mule to come beside him, then, one after the other, he broke off the arrows. If the mule had been disabled they would have lost food, camping equipment and, most important, their reserve stocks of carbine ammunition.

The wagon master knew then that so far they had been very lucky. They still had not learned all that he needed to know but they had some information to take back to Cookson. Under the circumstances it would be safer to postpone further enquiries until the army had chased away the hostiles. He knew that troops would already have been alerted and their arrival in the area was only a matter of time.

The mountains to the west were throwing long dark shadows across the landscape when the riders came in sight of the Overland Trail. It was hard to miss as thousands of wagons had passed that way since westward movement had commenced more than twenty years previously. They followed the trail for about half an hour until they reached the wheel tracks that passed for a road to Logjam Creek.

A couple of miles later Parry spoke to Murchison.

'It might be a good idea to stop and rest the horses for a while at Sullivan's Swamp,' he suggested. 'There's a campsite there that's easy to defend.'

'I know the place. Skinny Murphy's train had a big fight with some Arapahoes there in 'fifty-eight. I reckon I must know every campsite from Kansas to Idaho. We can stop there and, depending on how the horses are, we might head for Logjam Creek and travel through the night.'

Durango said nothing but he did not relish the prospect of another night sleeping on the ground, possibly with hostile Indians prowling about.

Kitty Page paused awhile and brushed her light-brown hair out of her eyes before lifting the family cooking utensils from the wagon. The scene around her was busy, as the occupants of the other three wagons were also setting up camp, but the girl felt a moment of peace. She loved the sound of the bells on the unyoked oxen as the hard-worked animals were turned loose to feed and rest. The bells were far from musical but their clattering announced that the day's journey was over.

Her father, Sandy, used to laugh at his daughter's concern for the animals that, for weeks, had moved their belongings slowly westward. Ever practical, Sandy had never neglected his animals but he had formed no close associations with them. His main concern, as the father of a very pretty daughter, was the Harper boys, John and Jesse, both of whom seemed smitten with Kitty.

21

Caleb Harper and his wife Betty were good travelling companions but he did not see either of their two poorly educated sons as a prospective member of the Page family. John was nineteen and Jesse seventeen; both were big rowdy teenagers, good-natured and willing workers but with more than a few rough edges for future life still to wear off them. Mary Page was of similar mind to her husband.

At this moment she was building a fire for their evening meal. She was tired of travelling and was eagerly looking forward to having a house and a proper kitchen of her own. She looked up to see her daughter looking into the fading light.

'Come on, young lady,' she said, trying to sound stern. 'Bring those pots over here and fill the kettle from the water barrel. We need to get set up properly before it gets too dark.'

A short distance away three men travelling with two of J.B. Cookson's freight wagons were also setting up camp. There were two teamsters, Marty Timms and Dave Hutchins, men who had hauled freight along western trails all through the Civil War. The third member was Paul Hockley, a former soldier working his way west. The teamsters had hired him when their previous assistant had refused to leave a trading post where, until his money was spent, there had been an assured supply of whiskey.

The four wagons had left the main train for the much fainter trail to Logjam Creek. Sandy Page had been hired by Cookson to set up and operate a sawmill and the Harper family had hoped to find employment

22

in the new town that was the centre of Cookson's expanding empire. As all wagons were drawn by oxen they kept together for safety's sake.

There had been vague stories about Indian problems but the journey thus far had been uneventful. An army patrol had informed them on the night before they turned off the main trail that they had seen no signs of Indians. As they went about their final tasks for the night the tired, hungry travellers gave little thought to warlike tribesmen.

Dave Hutchins was not a tall man and he cursed as he struggled to reach into the grub box on the side of his wagon and grope around for the sole remaining onion he had been saving for the night's stew. Timms laughed at his fellow teamster's efforts.

'You should ask J.B. to have the grub box attached a bit lower on your wagon,' he chortled.

'Shut that hairy face of yours, Marty, and get the potatoes out of your wagon. With that turkey that Hockley shot we should eat well tonight.'

Timms, seeing that the campfire was beginning to burn strongly, stood up and stretched his lanky frame.

'Just think of it, Dave,' he said, 'this time in two days we should be home at Logjam Creek. You'll be eating with Eileen and your two kids and I'll be throwing down a couple of drinks at Monson's saloon.'

Hockley was younger than the teamsters and envied those who looked forward to predictable futures. His clothes were showing the weeks of hard wear and he possessed less than two dollars in small change, the last of his army pay. His gaunt features and skinny frame showed that he had been surviving on one meal a day until the freighters had taken him on to replace their drunken roustabout.

At least he could eat regularly again. He was reluctant to reach the end of the journey because there was no guarantee that he would find paying work. Timms and Hutchins were good company but, apart from providing meals, they were unsure whether Cookson was prepared to pay him for his services.

The pair had found him to be useful in the camp and on several occasions he had borrowed Hutchins's double-barrelled shotgun and brought in game. Sometimes there had been enough to share with the Harpers and the Pages, but he felt awkward in a family environment and spent most of his short periods of spare time with the teamsters.

He was helping Hutchins peel potatoes when he heard one of the Harper boys call:

'Hey, Pa. There's riders comin'.'

Parry saw the campfires burning brightly against the full darkness that had at last descended. His companions also saw them and Murchison chuckled.

'Our luck's in. Looks like there's some wagons camped at the swamp. That should tip the odds in our favour if our scalp-hunting friends are still following.'

'Maybe not,' Parry said cautiously. 'It's possible that those Cheyennes were on their way to attack the train and met us only by accident. There were enough of those Dog Soldiers to cause a lot of grief if that train happens to be a small one.'

Durango disagreed. 'They've lost the element of surprise. Surely any attack would be too costly.'

'Don't bet your life on it,' Murchison warned. 'If they are still on our trail you can bet your boots they'll scout the camp tonight. Depending on what they find they might try to run off some of the stock or they might hit us first thing in the morning. They might even do both.'

'Who's there?' a voice called from the wagon camp.

'I'm Joe Murchison,' Murchison shouted back. 'Tom Parry and Durango Finch are with me.'

'Come in, Joe,' Timms bellowed. 'There's two of us Cookson wagons here and some other folks as well. We're all headed for Logjam Creek.'

The trio rode into the camp and dismounted. There were brief introductions all round, then Murchison cut them short.

'We could have a Cheyenne war party on our heels,' he warned. 'Let's start fortifying the camp because we don't know how close they might be.'

Hutchins almost swore, then remembered that ladies were present.

'Dang it, Joe! Did you have to bring them down on us?'

'Could be they were comin' after you anyway and we just happened to run into them first,' Parry told him. 'We can talk later.'

The news brought mixed reactions. The women were understandably nervous but the Harper boys, in their youthful ignorance, were looking forward to trying out the second-hand Navy Colts their father had bought for them. The older men did not share their enthusiasm because Cookson's teamsters had seen similar situations before. The adult men who had never fought Indians previously had seen military service in the Civil War and were not eager for the killing to start again.

Murchison was a veteran of confrontations with Indians and he took over reorganizing the camp.

The teams had been released to graze; now they had to be brought into the improvised corral formed by the four wagons together with ropes and chains attached to some of the trees on the campsite. The two Harper boys each strapped on a loaded revolver and caught their ponies. Within minutes they had the draught oxen and two ponies belonging to Cookson's men and the Page family safely in the enclosure.

Murchison unpacked the mule, adding its pack to a defensive breastwork and using the animal to drag a couple of logs into gaps in the defences. He took the time to extract two boxes of Winchester ammunition before arranging the pack in position. He knew that every Cookson wagon carried a Winchester or Henry repeater and he passed out a good supply of cartridges to every man who had such a weapon.

A strong chain was fastened between a wagon wheel and a tree and the horses were all securely tied there. It was anticipated that there would be some casualties among them because nowhere inside the flimsy defences was really safe. Using the shovels that every wagon carried, shallow trenches were scraped beneath the wagons. In these the defenders would be less likely to be trampled by any terrified or wounded oxen.

The back of the camp was on the edge of the swamp. No mounted attackers could approach from that direction and it would be difficult for dismounted men to move through it silently. Hockley with a shotgun and the two Harper boys, one with a shotgun and the other with a muzzle-loading rifle as well as their six-shooters, were to cover that approach. They were concealed beneath one of Cookson's big wagons.

The other freight wagon had part of its cargo moved to form a bullet-proof barrier on its outward-facing side. The three women would take shelter there, safely away from trampling stock and protected as much as possible from stray bullets. Page and Hutchins, both with repeating rifles, would defend this post.

Murchison and Timms with their Winchesters positioned themselves under the smaller Harper wagon; Durango and Parry were to place themselves under the Page wagon.

Full buckets of water were positioned under each wagon in case fire arrows were shot into the canvas canopies.

Before settling down Parry crept around to the other positions and in whispers warned the others not to betray their positions by shooting at shadows. He told them that the Cheyennes would probably scout the defences but, seeing the stock secure, they would not attack until dawn unless they found that the sentries were negligent.

He had just returned to his post when, out in the darkness a wolf howled, an eerie, lonely sound. A few seconds passed and another called from the opposite side.

'They've arrived,' he whispered to Durango. 'Those wolf howls are scouts talking to each other. They're trying to find out how many of us there are. They won't make a full-scale night attack because they are superstitious about fighting in the dark. But if they see the chance of collecting an easy scalp, or stealing horses, they might take a few risks, so don't relax.'

'As if I could under these circumstances,' the gunman muttered quietly.

The wagon teams started stirring and shuffling about as they picked up the unfamiliar scent. Some snorted, others bellowed low and anxiously The men manning the defences peered into the gloom fearful that already warriors could be creeping stealthily into close quarters.

THREE

Dawn came slowly and the defenders were yawning and gritty-eyed. The corralled cattle had been restless all night and consequently there had been little chance of anyone dozing off.

Vague shapes in the gloom now assumed identifiable outlines and dark shadows became colours. The first feeble rays of the sun glittered off the early-morning dew. Apprehension, like the visibility, increased with every passing minute.

The boom of a shotgun jolted the waiting defenders out of their sleep-deprived lethargy. The corralled livestock bellowed uneasily and began circling the enclosure that held them. More shots came from a collection of firearms and then, above the din, a chorus of spine-chilling war cries arose from the swamp behind the camp.

'They're behind us!' Durango twisted around as he spoke and tried to see through the legs of the moving cattle.

'It's only a diversion,' Parry shouted. 'They can't

charge through that swamp. Watch your front. While you can hear those shotguns they aren't getting inside.'

The breech-loading shotguns were keeping up a steady rate of fire that could be distinguished from reports of other firearms, but it was disturbing to know that the attackers were in such close range to the defences.

Arrows from concealed warriors were starting to strike the ground in front of the defensive rifle pits that were covering the open space from which the main attack was expected. Hidden in the long grass, the warriors would spring up, let loose their shafts, then drop back out of sight. A few arrows lodged their points in the wagon sides but, with no cloud of powder smoke to betray them, the number of archers was difficult to estimate.

Gunfire was soon coming from all around the camp's perimeter. The cattle were rushing about in panic, hitting wagons and sometimes shaking them alarmingly with the impact. Parry was hoping that none of the stock would break out of the flimsy enclosure that confined them because he knew that the expected assault could be masked by dust and frantic stock.

Suddenly the wagon cattle became the least of his problems. A group of mounted warriors surged out of a distant pine thicket, urging their ponies at a racing pace straight for the front of the camp. In seconds they were within range.

'Here they come,' Durango muttered. 'There's a heap of them.'

Parry had seen similar attacks before and knew that

mounted men looked more than their actual numbers. Despite this the usual doubt sprang to his mind. Did the defenders have enough guns to stop them? He fought down the first rush of nerves, pushing the anxiety from his mind. They had always been stopped before, he told himself. If he kept calm and shot straight today's result would be no different from previous encounters.

Someone under one of the other wagons began a rapid fire but Parry would not shoot blindly into the mass of horsemen. He selected his targets carefully. He squeezed the trigger and saw the man he had targeted smashed from his horse.

Beside him he heard Durango's rifle firing as quickly as its single-shot action would allow. He concentrated on his next target and did not check on Durango's victims. He thought he saw a horse go down, then his view was blotted out by a rider who loomed out of the dust. The warrior actually halted his pony a few paces from the wagon, shrieked out a war cry and, rifle in hand, jumped from his mount. As he hit the ground, he toppled over and landed right in front of Parry. The young man stared into the warrior's painted face and thrust his rifle against his attacker's fringed buckskin shirt.

The Cheyenne looked dazed and seemed to stare in horror at his own weapon as the white man fired. The close-range impact of the heavy bullet half-lifted its victim and rolled him on his side.

Parry knew his man was dead or dying and he looked around for another target. Through a haze of dust and powder smoke he saw Durango with a six-shooter in each hand, methodically firing into a whirling mass of Cheyennes. Gunfire was drowning out any war cries but it was obvious that the charging Indians had not broken into their makeshift fortress.

A couple of braves rode to the weak spots in the defensive barriers and tried to force their ponies through. Parry accounted for the one closest to him but the other turned away, disappearing into the cloud of churned-up dust and gun smoke.

The eleven rounds in Parry's carbine were spent in seconds but the Winchester's big advantage was that it was not out of action while being reloaded. At every lull between targets he was able to slip another cartridge or two through its loading port. He lost count of the bullets left in the magazine but knew he could keep the weapon in action.

The defenders in the other wagons were still throwing a lot of lead but the dust outside their position was beginning to clear.

The war cries had ceased as the wild riders were now concentrating on the task of picking up their dead and wounded. The living were lifted between two riders and carried from the field but the dead were simply secured by a rawhide rope and dragged away.

A few warriors rode about giving covering fire but their shooting was ineffectual against the entrenched white men.

Kitty cautiously raised her head above the additional reinforcing inside the wagon. The bedding and boxes and spare clothing had trapped the bullets that penetrated the wagon's sides but the canvas wagon cover had a few holes where bullets had torn through. One hole made by a large slug of some kind now made a convenient spy hole. She peered through and saw a couple of dead horses, but a dust cloud in the distance was the only sign of their late attackers.

'They're gone,' she told the two older women; she felt more than a little surprised that her voice was strangely shaky. 'We can get out and stretch our legs.'

'Keep your head down,' her pale-faced mother said sharply. 'Bullets can travel a long way. Stay right where you are until you hear it is safe to come out.'

Betty Harper, deeply concerned for her family, called down through the wagon floor:

'Mr Page, do you know if anyone's been hurt?'

'I don't know,' Page replied as he reloaded his weapons, 'but you'd best keep under cover until we see how the land lies.'

Parry called to his companions:

'I'll check on the others and let you know as soon as those cattle settle down so I won't get trampled. Best if everyone stays put for a while – and don't forget to reload your guns.'

As the oxen were gradually stopping their nervous circling of the corral Parry slipped out of his trench and examined the dead warrior who lay only a couple of feet away.

His victim was in a contorted position and showed no sign of life but a strong familiar odour clung to his body.

'Whiskey,' Parry said to Durango. 'This son of a gun was drunk. No wonder he fell over when he jumped off his pony. He smells as though he was swimming in booze.'

Then a closer look revealed a broken glass bottle inside the warrior's shirt. Parry's bullet had broken the bottle as it tore its way into the man's heart. The spilled whiskey, mingled with the wide pool of blood, was soaking into the churned-up earth.

A Wesson carbine lay beside the dead man, the action open to show a copper cartridge case in the breech. The carbine had two trigger guards and the warrior had made a mistake that was common with such a weapon. He had pulled the front trigger used for loading and unloading. Whether the fatal mistake had been caused by panic or whiskey Parry did not care. He was alive and that was all that mattered.

'Keep an eye out, Durango. I think those cattle have settled down enough for me to get through them and check on the others.' He raised his voice and shouted. 'Everyone, wait where you are a little longer just in case the Cheyennes come back.'

Caleb Harper was in no mood to take orders from someone half his age; he was already working his way to the back of the camp to check on his sons. He had heard his wife's voice and knew that she was unharmed.

Parry was too busy to worry about Harper disregarding his advice as he was more concerned about wounded Indians who might be lying in the grass. He found four dead ponies and several patches of blood where dead or wounded warriors had been removed and satisfied himself that no raiders were lurking near by.

The body of the drunken Indian whom he had killed was too close to the defenders' guns and was the only one left on the field. He collected the Wesson carbine and found another half-dozen rounds of ammunition for it in the warrior's pouch. He would give the weapon to Hockley for him to keep or sell as he made his way westward.

'It's safe,' he called. 'They're all gone.'

The defenders emerged, some elated but others looking nervously about them. Then they began to talk, swapping experiences with anyone who was prepared to listen. The two Harper boys were quite convinced that they had fought off hordes of savages but Hockley, who had been with them, said nothing. He had seen too much killing and was travelling west to distance himself from the grim memories of Eastern slaughters.

Murchison was shaking his head in disbelief. As a veteran of several Indian fights he was still amazed by the Cheyennes' attempt to make a mounted charge against entrenched enemies with repeating rifles. Some of the other defenders were of the same opinion.

'I reckon most of 'em must have been drunk,' Timms said.

The others saw no need to contradict him. The attack might have succeeded in the muzzle-loader days but cartridge weapons had replaced slow-loading firearms. The Indians' ability to keep up rapid streams of arrows was no longer an advantage against the faster-firing, more powerful guns of the white men.

As the cattle settled down a couple were found to have minor bullet wounds and another, more badly injured, would need to be shot. None of the horses had been wounded as they had been mostly shielded by the team animals as they milled around in the centre of the camp.

Kitty cautiously climbed down from the wagon just as Parry stopped near by to look at a bullet-damaged spoke in a rear wheel.

'Is it seriously damaged, Mr Parry?'

'I don't think so but I'm no expert on wheels. One of the teamsters will know for sure.' He paused, then said, 'There's no need to call me "mister". My first name is Tom. After what we've been through this morning, I think we can forget the formality.'

'A good idea. I'm Kitty. I must see if my pony is all right. He's that little sorrel over there.'

'The horses are fine. I checked them all when I was looking at that strawberry roan horse of mine. They were partly shielded by the wagon cattle. Some of them will need a bit of attention.'

'What happens now about resuming our journey?'

'I'll leave the others to organize that. The most useful thing I can do is to take a ride around and make sure those Cheyenne dog soldiers really are high-tailing it. We don't want them coming back again when the wagons are on the move.'

Kitty watched as Parry led out his horse and started saddling it.

'I like your horse, Tom,' she said. 'What do you call him?'

'Aubrey – it rhymes with strawberry. I know it's a funny name but I couldn't think of anything better at the time.'

'I think it is a very nice name, rather dignified.'

Parry laughed as he eased up the cinch.

'Stand still, Aubrey,' he said, 'none of that undignified behaviour.'

Kitty looked serious. 'Isn't it dangerous – going out there on your own, looking for Indians?'

'Only if they are still there – and I don't think that is very likely. There were not enough of them to attack us when we were forted up. They were either drunk or crazy.'

Kitty looked puzzled. 'Where would Indians get strong drink out here?'

'There are plenty of people who are prepared to sell liquor to the Indians in exchange for furs, valuable loot and stolen money. Quite a few hostiles know that white man's money is valuable when they are trading. Please excuse me now. I have to be sure the Cheyennes have really gone.'

Parry need not have worried, because a short way from the camp, he met a cavalry troop hurrying towards the sound of the gunfire.

Their middle-aged captain rode back to the camp and briefly heard the accounts of the battle. Excited that his men were so close to the hostiles, he was in no mood to waste time. He selected a corporal and six men whose horses were not suited for a long chase.

These were left to escort the wagons to Logjam Creek. Then, with two Osage scouts riding ahead, the troop set off in eager pursuit.

Murchison watched them go, then turned to Parry.

'No need for us here now. Time to go. J.B. won't be too happy with our news but that's too bad. He might not want us to keep huntin' Harker but he does get mighty single-minded at times.'

Timms joined them at this point.

'Homer Ewart will get a bit of work when we get to Logjam Creek,' he said. 'There's a few splintered boards on our two wagons and maybe a wheel needs replacing. The big slugs in some of those Indian muzzle-loaders have split a few side boards.'

'That won't worry Homer,' Murchison said confidently.' Setting up the company's own coachbuilder at headquarters had been one of Cookson's smarter moves. 'He can get repairs done *pronto* and keep his wagons on the road. I'll go ahead with Durango and Tom now that you have an army escort.'

'See you in Logjam,' Timms said, and walked back to his wagon.

FOUR

Wilf Bonner hunched over the wagon seat and resisted the urge to drive faster. He had just killed a man and wanted to get clear of Logjam without attracting attention before the body was discovered.

Bonner's extensive criminal career had been successful because he looked so ordinary that people rarely noticed him. A man of medium height and build, he was in his late thirties. He sometimes altered his appearance according to the fashions in various localities. Judging by the battered grey hat on his head and his dusty boots he could have been any one of many frontier workers.

Like many frontiersmen he wore a big revolver on his right hip, but the rather battered weapon was mostly for show. He had killed the coachbuilder at close range with a small .32 revolver that he had drawn left-handed from under his unbuttoned coat. A couple of men had died because he had drawn the hideout weapon while his victims were not suspecting that he was reaching for a gun.

Bad luck, he told himself. How was he to know that the coachbuilder had recognized the stolen wagon he was driving? Bonner had quietly collected a few boxes of empty bottles and a small keg of whiskey from the rear of Monson's saloon when he stopped at the coach-maker's to see about replacing a broken catch on the wagon's tailboard. A considerable effort had been made to disguise the prairie schooner. It was mud-spattered and its canvas cover was torn and rotting, but the tradesman had recognized his own handiwork immediately.

He had given no thought to the consequences when he asked Bonner how he had acquired the vehicle. At close range the small cartridge was not noisy and the workshop was on the edge of town away from houses. Homer Ewart's misfortune had been to open his business premises at a time when most people were just having their breakfast.

Cookson was not in a good mood when Murchison knocked on the door of his home late at night. His heavily lined face changed from serious to grim when he saw the wagon master. They had been close friends for decades and his usual cheery greeting was noticeably absent. He ushered Murchison into what passed as a living room in his spartan accommodation and indicated a chair.

Normally he would have produced a whiskey bottle and a couple of glasses, but not this time. He seated himself in a well-worn chair and went straight to business.

'What have you found, Joe? What's happening about Harker?'

Murchison explained but his boss seemed distracted and not really to be paying much attention to his report.

'That's the situation,' Murchison concluded. 'We probably need to go back and have another look at the tracks we found now the army has the Cheyennes on the run.'

Cookson's hard blue eyes narrowed behind his wire-framed spectacles; he spoke quietly.

'You might not need to go too far from here,' he said, 'because it looks like Ollie was in town here yesterday. Could be he killed Homer Ewart. His assistant found him dying when he turned up for work. He lived just long enough to say something about Harker. He seemed determined to let people know but could just get the name out.'

'Hell, J.B.! Ewart and Harker were good friends. I can't imagine them falling out to the extent that one killed the other. Did anyone else see or hear anything?'

'Someone heard an old rattletrap wagon early but Harker's wagon was a good one and always in good order.'

Murchison disagreed. 'The last I saw of it, it was a pile of ashes. I prodded around thinking I might find Harker's remains underneath but I only found a few of the iron fittings. Some hostile Indians arrived about then so we could not examine the scene as much as we would have liked. Do you want us to go back for another look?'

Cookson thought for a few moments.

'Ewart's murder has changed things a bit,' he then replied. 'I want you to stay here and ask around town. Someone must have seen or heard something. It's hard for me to accept but I think Harker might have betrayed my trust and it's likely he killed Ewart.'

'Damnit J.B.!' Murchison made no attempt to hide the frustration in his voice. 'Do you have to be so secretive about everything? You know something that you ain't tellin' me? Why would Harker kill Ewart? What's goin' on?'

'These are lawless times, Joe; there is no law here for a hundred miles at least and the same applies to banks. When it comes to large sums of money I tell only the people involved – and even then only if I trust them. I limit what I tell them to what they need to know.'

'And you reckoned I didn't need to know? You trusted Harker before me?'

'You would have been told, Joe, as soon as Harker reached Logjam Creek. I would never have expected him to go bad. Just shows what a lot of money can do to a man.'

'How much money are you talkin' about, J.B.?'

'Thousands. Running costs and wages. There are no banks out here, nor is there a coach line. This town is just starting. At present the safest way to move money is to keep it secret. Harker was not told how much but he must have guessed it was a lot.'

'But why would he kill Ewart? They were good friends.'

'That's what I want you to find out. Get Tom Parry to

go back to the remains of the wagon and see what he can find. Send Finch with him. That man is a hired gun and we don't want him sniffing around here and picking up the scent of money. Some of those characters can change sides very quickly.'

Murchison stood up and was about to leave when a thought suddenly struck him.

'What if someone found out about the money and took the whole shebang to find it?'

Cookson shook his head vigorously. 'That wouldn't happen, Joe. The only people who knew about the deal were the bank where the money was dished out, Harker and myself. With Ewart's murder things don't look good for Ollie Harker. If he's alive and has nothing to hide why hasn't he come forward? And where in the hell is my money?'

Parry did not mind being sent out again but Durango was far from happy. He had been drinking and playing poker at Monson's saloon most of the previous night. Now tired, hung over and thirty-five dollars poorer, the gunman dozed in his saddle. He could see no reason why he should have been sent back to the remains of Harker's wagon with Parry but now he was short of ready cash and needed to stay on Cookson's payroll a little longer.

Parry had decided that instead of following their previous course they should ride cross-country to the burnt wagon. Even though the terrain would be rougher in some places they would save a full day's travel. Their route took them first along Logjam Creek where willows and cottonwoods shielded them from the early morning sun; but after an hour's ride the creek turned in the wrong direction. They paused briefly to give their horses a drink because the next part of their journey would involve a long, waterless climb over a steep mountain range.

The trees gradually thinned as the horses fought their way up increasingly steep inclines. Sometimes their hoofs dislodged small rocks, creating tiny avalanches of gravel and pine needles. At the edge of the tree line Parry called a halt in order to rest their mounts.

Durango was feeling a little better as he looked back from the heights. He could see the winding course of Logjam Creek and, far to the west, small plumes of chimney smoke rising from the general area of the town. Turning slightly he saw Parry looking south with a small brass telescope.

'Looking for Indians, Tom?'

'No. I'm looking at the wagons that we fought with the other night. I can just make out the four of them. They'll be in town by nightfall.'

Durango gave one of his rare smiles.

'You wouldn't be looking for Kitty Page, would you? The two of you seemed to be getting along well in the short time you had together.'

'She's easy to get along with, that's all. She's like that with everyone. She even told me that she thought you were a nice man. Have you ever thought of settling down?'

'Before the war I probably did but it's best not to

complicate my current business with a wife and family.
Most men in this trade don't reach old age. They don't
get killed by other gunfighters: they are mostly shot
down from ambush without a chance to draw a gun.
Some become lawmen but they don't last long. Some
are shot by drunks and some change sides and fall foul
of the law. Very few grow old and grey at this game.'

'You could easily give it up.'

Durango shook his head. 'I can't agree with you
there. You make enemies and they know where to find
you.' He paused for a while, as if he had said too much,
then he added with a rueful smile, 'But I must admit
that the hours are short and the money is good.'

They remounted and urged their horses up to the
stony barren crest of the range. There was no snow but
a chilly breeze was blowing. The perspiration had
soaked their shirts on the climb, now it turned cold
and the two men were not tempted to linger and
admire the view.

Parry delayed only long enough to run his telescope
over the scene ahead. He could not see their objective
because of the pine trees and cedars on the lower
slopes but he satisfied himself that the wagon's remains
would be easy to locate. As he was putting his telescope
away he saw a faint puff of white smoke swirl among the
tree tops before dissipating in the erratic breeze that
seemed to be blowing on the eastern side.

'I just saw some smoke,' he said. 'It wasn't a signal,
the day is too windy. I doubt it would be Indians. They
don't light fires in daytime when they're running from
the army. Might be an old trapper; there are still a few

of them around.'

Durango pointed at a hill across the valley into which they were about to descend.' I saw it just then – over on that hill to the north-east. Is that where we are heading?'

'No – not unless a trail leads us that way, but if we don't find anything else we could have a look to see what's there.'

They rode south for a couple of miles along the rocky spine of the range before starting the descent to the valley below. It was afternoon and the eastern side of the range was already in deep shadow. When they entered the trees the gloom increased. In the stillness the hoofbeats of the horses seemed strangely loud. It was getting difficult to see and both riders suffered scratches from low branches that they only saw at the last minute.

At last they emerged on to a small grassy flat beside a shallow creek. As they allowed their horses to drink Parry pointed to the mud at the water's edge. The hoof-prints of several ponies showed clearly in the damp soil.

'Someone else was here fairly recent. Could be those Cheyennes we tangled with. They probably scattered to get away from the soldiers.'

'What if they are still here somewhere?' Durango asked, looking nervously about him. 'We made enough noise coming down the mountain to notify every Indian in the valley.'

'I reckon they're long gone,' Parry said. 'Those tracks are about two days old. Let's find a nice sheltered campsite somewhere in these trees and settle down for the night. We ain't eaten since morning and my belt buckle is rubbing blisters on my backbone.'

'That's the best suggestion I have heard today,' Durango said in a tired voice.

FIVE

They staked out their horses on a patch of good grass and lit a small fire to provide light while they prepared a meal from the contents of their saddlebags. It was basic: just a couple of slices of not-quite-stale bread and cold roast beef washed down with coffee made in tin cups. Breakfast would be much the same except that the last remaining bread would be really stale and there would be no coffee. Parry had decided that a campfire in the morning might attract unwelcome attention.

Durango was not impressed. As he chewed at the unappetizing fare he paused between mouthfuls.

'You weren't joking when you said we would be travelling light. No wonder you are as skinny as a Mexican's dog.'

Parry laughed. 'We can move a lot quicker without a pack mule. But enjoy the good grub because tomorrow we will only have jerky and a couple of ship's biscuits.'

'That's bad enough,' Durango complained, 'but

sleeping on a gum poncho under a sweaty saddle blanket is downright inhuman. I thought I was done with that when the war ended.'

'At least you've had practice at it. Nobody will find us here tonight so you should be able to get a good sleep.'

Next morning both were awake before sunrise. Durango had not slept very well and the cold hard ground had left him chilled and aching.

Breakfast, such as it was, did not take long and within half an hour of awaking they were on their way. Parry led as they emerged from the forest and crossed the broad flat valley floor. A small herd of deer fled for the safety of the trees and a couple of coyotes slunk away in the sagebrush as they sighted the horsemen.

The pair had no trouble finding the remains of the wagon but any useful tracks had been obscured by the passage of both cavalry and Indians over the area. Some riders had even ridden through the cold ashes of the fire and scattered them. Parry rode about the scene but learned nothing from it.

'There's nothing here,' he said. 'I want to have a look past the point where those Indians turned up the other day. If we find nothing else, we might try to see who is making that smoke.'

Durango stood in his stirrups and looked ahead.

'Can't see any sign of smoke now.'

'At this level the tall trees would hide it. That fire, whatever it is, was planned by someone who was not keen on having visitors. It could be some old mountain man but one thing is certain: anyone who has been living here might have a good idea of what happened to Harker.'

'Assuming they are prepared to talk,' Durango observed pessimistically. 'Some of these old loners don't like strangers.'

Modoc Willie emerged from the sod-roofed dugout built into the steep hillside, his Henry repeater in the crook of his arm, hunting on his mind. Inside, his partners Wilf Bonner and Henry Crane were still sleeping off the effects of sampling their latest distillation. All three had agreed that the raw liquor would have to be an acquired taste but the Indians would not mind. They had never known the taste of good whiskey.

The half-breed had not consumed as much as his two associates and was feeling quite energetic as he made his way through the untidy, junk-cluttered camp to where their still was located. The fire under the boiler was still alight but he added another wooden block to it just to make sure it didn't go out before he returned.

With this last task over, he checked the loads in his rifle and stepped quietly into the surrounding forest. They were running low on meat and Willie enjoyed hunting more than he enjoyed moonshining. Keeping in the timber, he worked his way to a low ridge that would give him a good view of the more open country where he was sure he would find a fat buck to replenish their food supply.

Something far down the plain caught his attention, something shiny that was catching the rays of the newly risen sun. A closer glance revealed two distant horse-men. The nearer horse was a large, black animal and as it walked the sunlight was just at the right angle to reflect off shiny conchos on its saddle.

Any hunting would have to wait. Modoc Willie turned in his tracks and started running back to the sod hut. Intruders spelt trouble and his partners in crime had to be warned.

As Parry and Durango moved up the valley they had a clear view of the smoke rising from a patch of forest ahead of them on their right.

'Looks like someone is home,' Durango observed. 'They should be able to tell us something.'

They rode closer; then suddenly Parry pointed ahead.

'I can see wagon tracks going up that slope over there. They're fresher than any of the other tracks. We would have seen them if they came from the same direction as us.'

'Could they get here from any other direction?' Durango asked.

'There's a trail goes round the north end of these mountains that leads to Logjam Creek. It's longer and rougher and very dangerous when Indians break out. Most folks would go the regular way.'

'Most folks would not worry about being seen,' the gunman went on. 'We might need to be careful in calling on whoever is keeping that fire burning. I saw a lot of moonshine operations over in the East and that continuous smoke is a trademark of these businesses.

51

Many a man who stumbled on a still never lived to tell of it. Moonshiners are mighty dangerous people.'

' 'Specially when they sell that rotgut to the Indians,' Parry agreed.

The half-breed found his two companions awake and half-dressed when he burst through the hut door.

'Strangers headin' this way – two of 'em – could be the law,' he panted before they could say a word.

There was a scramble for hats, boots and weapons as Bonner and Crane forgot their hangovers.

'Get up to the flat rock,' Crane grunted, stamping his feet into his boots. 'We can't see enough from here.'

In hiding their operation the moonshiners had compromised their own view of its approaches, but a big slab of rock on rising ground was less than a hundred paces away and it allowed a good view down the trail to the shack. A thin screen of trees growing in front of the slab meant that their vantage point was well concealed.

The trio were just stretching out on the rock when they saw the two riders approaching. Both were looking warily about them as they rode and one of them on a roan horse had a drawn Winchester carbine in his right hand. The early-morning sun was glancing off a big, nickel-plated revolver held by the other rider, on a black horse. The riders were widely separated to make more difficult targets.

'This pair know what they're doing,' Bonner whispered to his companions.

The pair halted near the sod shack but at such an

angle that they could not be fired upon by anyone inside. Durango hailed a greeting to anyone who might be in the vicinity but no response came to his call.

To the newcomers the silence in itself was ominous and both men sensed that they were being watched. A wagon with a tattered canopy was parked under trees on their left. A faint path beside it led into the trees; Parry was sure that it would lead to a hidden pasture for wagon teams or riding-horses. Directly in front there appeared to be a thin screen of trees while to their right stood a sod hut and a lean-to with a chimney. The lean-to had no door and they could see that a large metal boiler was set over a fire.

'Someone's watching us for sure,' Durango said quietly. 'Best we get off these horses. If you want to look around I'd better stay here and watch for any trouble. Be careful. Keep in sight of me and don't stand in the one place too long.'

Parry dismounted and handed his reins to Durango, who was already on the ground looking warily about. But the gunslinger had no intention of making himself an easy target; he moved between the two horses who afforded him some protection.

After taking a deep breath, and hoping that Durango would see any danger in time, Parry went first to the wagon. His boots clinked on broken glass that was scattered in the grass near by. A glance through a tear on the canvas showed him all he needed to see. There were a few boxes and some bottles, all empty. A pile of harness and a battered saddle were at the end behind the driver's seat. The tailboard was down but it hung crookedly because one of its hinges was broken. Parry had seen enough; he hurried back to where Durango was waiting.

'It's a whiskey-runner's outfit,' he said. 'Looks like they've been selling their stuff by the bottle. Most of these skunks sell it one tin cup at a time. It gets their customers drunk quicker. Those Cheyenne war parties probably gathered in this area because they knew there was whiskey for sale. I'll have a look at the soddy now.'

'Don't be too long about it. There's trouble here somewhere, I don't like this place at all,' urged Durango.

Parry made his approach from the windowless side of the shack to ensure that no one inside could take a shot at him. A glance at the dirt outside the door showed the tracks of three men leaving, two wearing boots and one wearing moccasins. Standing beside the entrance he called sharply:

'Is anyone in there?'

Silence.

After a few seconds of intent listening he took a chance, cocked his Winchester and jumped through the low doorway. Relief flooded through him as he saw no fourth man lurking with a gun in the single room. A pile of furs and buffalo robes did service as beds and a few items of clothing were strewn untidily on the dirt floor. A battered hat of cheap wool felt lay on a box. The brim was torn and limp and was pinned up in front with a horseshoe nail to keep it from falling over the wearer's eyes.

Parry picked it up and looked to see if there was a

name written on the sweatband. Seeing none, he dropped the hat and glanced around. A couple of old muzzle-loading rifles were propped in one corner and some wooden boxes held food and a few cooking utensils. Three men would find the shack cramped and uncomfortable, but it did offer some shelter against the rain and the wind.

Henry Crane, in his early fifties, was the oldest of the three moonshiners. He had a long and violent past going back to his days as an eager fighter in the Kansas-Missouri border wars before the Civil War. A cold and deliberate killer, he lay quietly peering over the sights of his rifle. Sooner or later the two intruders would come together and offer a good target.

Parry had seen enough in the soddy; now he went to the lean-to. He was not surprised to see the still. They were reasonably common on the frontier in places where strong liquor was hard to get. Supplying a few thirsty white men might be excused but trading it to the Indians was not. Liquor turned peaceful tribesmen into drunken savages and brought deadly conflict in its wake.

An axe for firewood lay near by so he set aside his rifle and used the axe to cut through the copper coil that channelled the alcoholic steam to where it cooled and became liquid again. The hot steam hissed through the ruptured pipe and the smell of moonshine filled the small structure. Seeing a spigot on the collecting tank, he opened it and a stream of strong-smelling liquid began pouring out. The smell drifted on the wind to the men on the rock.

'That sonofabitch has wrecked the still!' Crane swore when he realized what had happened. 'Open fire as soon as you can get a clear shot.'

The words were hardly out of his mouth when he glimpsed Parry hurrying towards the horses.

'Got you!' he said.

His finger began to apply pressure to the trigger.

SIX

Bonner's hand flashed out and a finger went between the rifle's descending hammer and the firing pin.

'*Don't*!' he hissed urgently in response to Crane's angry look of enquiry. 'Nobody shoot.'

'Why the hell not?'

'That big *hombre* with the horses – that's Durango Finch. He's hell on wheels with a gun. Unless you can drop him with your first shot some of us are gonna finish up dead. Chances are that that young coyote with him could be nearly as good.'

'Never heard of him,' Crane growled.

'I have,' Modoc Willie volunteered. 'He's called Durango because that's where he took on three pistoleros – killed 'em all inside about five seconds. Nobody there ever saw such shootin' before. The story is that he never misses a shot. One of the others managed to get one shot off but that missed anyway.'

'They're getting away,' Crane protested as he saw both riders mount.

Bonner suggested that they might get a clear shot as

57

the pair rode away. All agreed but then an argument ensued as to whether they should all concentrate on Durango or try to get both men with their initial volley.

The main objects of the moonshiners' attention unwittingly brought their argument to nothing.

'Best we get off this trail, Tom, just in case they try to back-shoot us,' suggested Durango. 'Get straight into the trees at the side.'

Parry needed no urging as he was thinking on similar lines. He wheeled Aubrey into the sheltering timber even as Durango left the trail.

Behind them the three would-be assassins pretended disappointment but secretly they were relieved that a potentially lethal situation had been averted.

'The boss ain't gonna like us lettin' that pair go,' Willie said.

'We can cook up some sort of story about being somewhere else when they came,' Bonner suggested.

'Do you think he'd fall for that?' Crane snarled back at him. 'He don't have much faith in us already since you had to kill that coachbuilder in Logjam. I can't believe you were dumb enough to take a stolen wagon back for repairs to the fella that made it.'

'How was I to know? I'm new to these parts and to me it don't look any different to heaps of other wagons. See one you've seen 'em all.'

'I'll see the boss in Logjam and find out what he wants to do now.' Crane was not too enthusiastic about his self-appointed task but knew that Bonner and Willie would have trouble putting together a plausible excuse for their failure. 'Meanwhile, pack up those furs and skins and hide them somewhere. They're worth a lot of money and we don't want to lose them if the army or the law come snooping.'

Aware that they were out of both range and sight of the moonshiners, Parry and Durango slowed their horses to a walk. After briefly discussing what they had found they turned their horses' heads to the north. They would pick up the tracks of the moonshiners' wagon and try to find where it had come from.

'So far we've found Indians and whiskey-runners,' Durango said, a note of exasperation in his voice, 'but we are supposed to be hunting Harker. I'm not sure if we have made any progress at all on that job.'

'Cookson won't be impressed if we come back empty-handed again.'

'Don't worry about him, *compadre*. He seems to be playing games too. There's a lot he hasn't told us. Are we looking for a wagon thief or the victim of foul play?'

Parry was looking around frequently as they rode. It paid to be cautious because friends in that particular area were hard to find but enemies seemed to be plentiful.

'I reckon that Cookson is looking for something more than a stolen wagon or a murdered driver. This search must have cost him nearly as much as the wagon and team were worth.'

Durango agreed and raised one more doubt.

'Didn't it strike you as odd that someone went to great lengths to make sure that that burnt wagon we found was almost totally destroyed?'

Parry was not looking for more complications but he had to admit that the gunman was right.

'It will be mighty interesting to follow up the tracks of the moonshiners' rig, but I'm still not sure that it has anything to do with Harker's disappearance.'

'We can say that we followed the trail in both directions and, apart from our moonshining friends, we found nothing. That's assuming that nothing unusual turns up on the way. Will we get back to town tonight?

'I want a good meal and a good sleep. As far as I'm concerned, all this fresh air should be kept outside where it belongs.'

Parry laughed. 'Sorry to disappoint you. The trail follows a winding route that would break a snake's back. We can stop overnight at a creek I know and if we get an early start, we should reach town about noon tomorrow.'

Durango groaned.

Darkness had fallen and lamps were appearing in the windows when Crane reached Logjam Creek. Astride a hardy, sure-footed mule, he had crossed the mountains along an old Indian trail that the moonshiners had been shown by their best customers. It was a useful short cut when no wheeled vehicles were needed.

Riding quietly, he attracted little attention. At that time of night most townspeople were preparing or eating meals. He saw no one as he turned into the alley that led to the back of Monson's saloon but he knew that he was under observation.

Al Webber would be watching from an upstairs

balcony and he would have a sawn-off shotgun under his arm. He was Monson's bodyguard and was constantly supervising the comings and goings at the saloon's back entrance. Harmless customers entered from the street but the more dubious visitors who preferred not to be seen used the rear door. The saloon had been held up once and its owner was taking precautions against anything similar happening again.

More than six feet in height and solidly built, Webber was a powerful man who could handle drunks, would-be hold-up men or anyone else who was likely to trouble his boss. He had the scarred face and crooked nose of a prize-fighter and his age could have been anywhere between thirty-five and fifty. On the odd occasion when gunplay was necessary he had proved to be a deadly shot with the pair of converted open-top Colts that he wore.

Before Durango arrived Webber had been the only two-gun man in town. The ease of loading afforded by metallic cartridges had greatly reduced the need for a second gun but he still felt that the extra firepower justified the weight and inconvenience.

Crane halted his mule and looked up at the dark figure staring over the balcony rail.

'Al, it's me, Henry Crane. I have to see the boss.'

'Hitch your mule to that post there. Monson's in his office. Just go on in.'

The saloon owner was seated in a comfortable chair in his office below a wall lamp that shone light on the week-old Denver newspaper that he was reading. He heard Crane's boots coming down the hall outside the office and knew that the visitor had been passed by Webber. Nevertheless, he slipped his right hand into a pocket concealed in the chair's upholstery. The newspaper on his lap disguised the hand gripping a small revolver. Monson trusted nobody.

'Come in,' he ordered when he heard Crane's knock.

A small, neat man with thinning grey hair, Monson seemed almost too inoffensive to run a frontier saloon but he had chosen his henchmen well and could command the necessary degree of violence when he wished.

'There's trouble at the still.' Crane did not bother with pleasantries.

'What's happened?'

As Crane recounted his story the frown on his boss's face deepened.

'Where were you three while these strangers were wrecking the still?' he asked in a tone that was harsh and very direct. 'I wanted someone to be there at all times.'

'There was a break in the fence at the mule pasture and some were missing. Modoc Willie thought Indians might have been trying to steal them. If that's what it was we would all need to be there. Turned out that a mule scratching itself had knocked over a rotten post and the missing ones were feeding only about half a mile away.'

'What happened then?'

'Willie and I got the mules back in and patched up the fence. Bonner went back to the still. We were on our way back when Bonner ran up and said two strangers, probably lawmen, were at the still. We hurried back but they were already riding away after wrecking the operation.'

'Do you know who they were?'

'Bonner said he thought one was that gunfighter Cookson hired recently. There was a younger one on a strawberry roan horse but none of us knew him.'

'I do,' Monson said. 'He works for Cookson too. They were hunting for Harker's wagon with Joe Murchison. Cookson is leaving no stone unturned to find Harker. Seems he was an old and trusted employee.'

'What do you want us to do now?'

'Keep clear of town. Bonner killed Ewart last week and people are asking why. Seems Ewart said something about Harker as he was dying. Some folks have jumped to the conclusion that Harker killed him and I am not discouraging that notion. There's no law here at present but some lawman will hear about the shooting eventually and come sniffing about. It is best that he should not know about you men.'

'What about the still? It could be put back into operation if we could get another copper coil.'

'Leave it. Get those furs and hides into the wagon and start it on the road to the rail station at Porter's Gulch as quick as you can. Our usual dealer in Chicago will arrange their sale. I have the cash here and will get it to a bank on my next trip East. Tell Willie that I want to see him as quick as he can get here. I think I can keep Cookson's men away from you while you are moving the furs.'

'What about the empty bottles that Crane had collected from here? There's still a couple of boxes of them. Can they be traced back to this saloon?'

'I'd clean forgot about them. Best if you hide them or even break and bury them – but do it somewhere away from the camp, where people won't notice any dug-up ground. We might need to keep away from that area until the fuss over Harker dies down.'

Relieved that Monson had not seriously questioned his version of events, Crane asked:

'What do you want me to do now?'

'Have a meal and a drink and bunk down in our stable. Webber will call you so you can be out of town before it gets light. I don't want anyone to know that we know each other.'

SEVEN

When the Page family arrived at Logjam Creek, they were allocated one of the several houses that Cookson had had constructed for some of his more senior employees. The previous occupier had moved on but had left behind a large ginger-and-white cat. The animal was smart enough to ingratiate himself immediately with Kitty and was promptly adopted. Soon he was sleeping on the foot of her bed.

Mary and Sandy had reluctantly agreed to Kitty's keeping the cat on condition that she looked after it. Among her duties was letting the animal out in the early hours of the morning, when it would stand at the door and meow loudly. This morning the drowsy girl opened the door as usual without showing any light and ushered the cat through.

A full moon was still high in the sky and by its silver beams the town's single street could be seen clearly. Monson's saloon was a hundred yards away on the opposite side of the street, casting dark shadows through the patches of moonlight.

Kitty was about to close the door when a movement

in the lane beside the saloon caught her eye. A man leading a saddled mule emerged from the shadows. Briefly he stood in the moonlight looking back into the lane, then another man appeared. For a few moments they appeared to be in conversation, then the first man mounted his mule and turned it down the street towards where Kitty was watching.

Quietly the girl pushed the door to, leaving it sufficiently ajar for her to see the approaching rider. He was seated comfortably on a fast-walking black mule. His face was partly shaded by his hat: a battered, very floppy arrangement with the front of the brim pinned up to keep it out of its owner's eyes. His facial details were indistinct but Kitty could discern a bushy beard. The only other noticeable feature was that the man wore a fringed buckskin coat.

Kitty watched with some curiosity until the rider was out of sight, then she returned to bed. Sleep reclaimed her while she was still wondering about the strange time of the traveller's departure.

Parry and Durango reached the town just before noon. At Cookson's freight depot they unsaddled and fed their mounts before turning them loose in one of the vacant corrals. They stowed their saddles and gear in the teamsters' bunkhouse and, after a quick wash, they were leaving to have a meal at the town's only restaurant when Murchison intercepted them.

'I wondered when you pair would be getting back,' the wagon master declared. 'What have you got to tell J.B.?'

'Nothing much at all,' Durango admitted.

'We found a still where those Cheyenne dog soldiers got likkered up before we had our fight with them at Sullivan's Swamp,' Parry told him. 'But there's no sign of Harker.'

Murchison looked disappointed. He scratched his chin for a second or two, then asked:

'Who was at the still?'

'We never saw anyone, but I have a feeling they were around,' Durango replied. He turned to Parry. 'You had a better look around than I did, Tom. What do you reckon?'

'Looked like three or four men were there. They had a lot of good furs and skins in the soddy where they lived, so they were trading with the Cheyennes. They probably had money there, too, but we had no time to look for it and we weren't sure that they would tell us anything about Harker even if they knew. I wrecked the still before we left, smashed the cooling coil, so they will be out of business for a while now.'

'Another visit might be worth while,' Durango suggested, 'but we need a few more men and some legal backing. Moonshiners are very dangerous people. Cookson might not want to get involved if Harker had nothing to do with them – and I can't say that I am all that eager either. Before the war I was a deputy sheriff in Tennessee and those moonshiners can be as dangerous as any of our Western badmen.'

'The boss is tied up with Sandy Page at present. They are working on the plans for the sawmill. I'll tell him what happened and see what he wants to do. Be ready to move out quickly if needs be. Stay around town so you can be found. J.B. likes to take his time and think things out but when his mind is made up he wants everything to happen pronto.'

Parry and Durango took their leave of the wagon master and hurried to the restaurant for the long-anticipated decent meal. After that they parted company. The gunman headed for Monson's saloon while Parry went to the corrals to check his horse's shoes. They were reasonably new but, with the prospect of further long rides, he liked to be sure that the nail clenches were still tight. They were: the recent hard travelling seemed to have caused no damage.

Satisfied that Aubrey was fit to go when needed, Parry dumped more of Cookson's hay into the manger attached to the corral rail and left the horse to munch undisturbed.

The Pages' house was near the freight depot. As he walked back Parry saw Kitty watering the few straggling plants that grew in the front yard behind the picket fence.

She looked up when he spoke and he was pleased to see the smile that lit up her pretty face. He had not been sure how his attentions would be received back in civilization – if Logjam Creek could be considered civilized.

'Hello, Tom. I wondered where you had gone.'

'Durango and I have been looking for Cookson's missing driver,' Parry replied. He thought it best not to say too much. 'Didn't have any luck, though. How are things with you?'

She smiled. 'We love it,' she said enthusiastically. 'After months of living in a wagon it is nice to have a house again. Pa is kept busy with Mr Cookson but he's enjoying his work. Paul Hockley and the Harper boys have found jobs as roustabouts and stock wranglers with the freight wagons. They will be away a lot.

'The Harpers are renting a house here and Caleb has been given a job helping to build the mill. They are just down the street a few houses away.'

'I hope you don't get too much noise from over the road,' Parry said, indicating the saloon. 'Some of Monson's customers are wild men when they get a few drinks aboard.'

'So far things are quiet. I think we are far enough away not to be too troubled.'

'Steer clear of it at busy times. A skinful of Monson's whiskey seems to bring out the worst in some men.'

'I saw one of his customers leaving the saloon when I was putting out the cat in the early hours of this morning. At first I thought he might have been creeping away without paying his bill but then I saw someone else talking to him.'

Parry's curiosity was stirred. Could it have been Harker?

'What did he look like?' he asked.

'It was hard to see his face properly but I saw a beard. He had a buckskin jacket and was riding a mule. He had a ragged old hat with the front pinned up. The moonlight glinted on something shiny and it could have been a pin of some sort – or even a nail – but I really can't imagine anyone mending a hat with a nail.'

Parry remembered the hat he had seen at the moonshiners' camp. There could not be two such hats. But
he did not want to embroil Kitty in what could be a very
dangerous game. They talked for a while and eventually the subject came around to horses. Kitty's sorrel
pony was showing his age and she enquired about the
cost of a replacement.

'There are plenty of mustangs and Indian ponies
about but a lot have been badly broken. Some Indian-
broke ones don't like white people, others are not used
to women, but if you get the right one they are good
value. Eight or ten dollars is the going price.'

'I had my heart set on a bigger horse, something like
your Aubrey.'

'He cost me sixty dollars but I needed a special sort
of a horse that could take a lot of hard work. Your
horse will never need to stand up to long travelling, big
weights and hard riding. If you are interested I know a
man who still buys a few ponies from the friendly
Indians.

'He experiments with breeding and is always trying
to breed the perfect horse, but with only a small ranch
he has to keep the horse numbers down. His name is
George Roberts and he lives only a couple of miles out
of town. He's honest too. If you like I could see if he
has anything that would suit you. It might have to be
broken to the side saddle, though.'

'That's no problem.' Kitty laughed. 'I have a divided
skirt and I ride astride, much to my mother's horror.
She thinks it is unladylike.'

'Good for you. Some side saddles are uncomfortable

for the horses and if a horse should happen to fall, the rider is often trapped in the saddle and badly hurt or even killed. If you like, Kitty, I can have a word with George Roberts. He's one of our local characters.'

An idea was already forming in Parry's mind but getting the right pony for Kitty was only part of it. George Roberts was a long-time resident of the district and was a fount of local knowledge. He was a man who kept to himself but he seemed to know about most of the comings and goings at Logjam Creek.

'He always has more horses than he needs because he is always trying to breed the perfect horse,' Parry went on. 'He has a good Morgan stallion but mostly gets his mares from the Indians. He makes sure, though, that he only gets good types and he's bred some nice ponies at times. I need to see him about another matter and was thinking of taking a ride out there tomorrow. I can see if he has a suitable pony for you that he wants to sell.'

'That would be nice,' Kitty said. 'Mr Cookson allows his employees to run their own horses with those that his company keeps in town. My parents are willing to buy me a new horse but they're worried about some of the mad mustang types that we see around.'

'Don't worry. I'll make sure that it is well-behaved. Nobody wants to see you get smashed up.'

With that assurance Parry departed, feeling pleased with himself. He had an excuse to see more of Kitty and a reason to visit George Roberts.

EIGHT

'Just the man I wanted to see,' was Roberts's hearty greeting when Parry rode up to his front porch. 'Step down and come inside.'

It was a while since the pair had last met and Parry was surprised to see how much the old former cowhand had aged. What hair he had left was white, he had lost weight and developed a pronounced stoop. He lived alone in a small cabin that was surprisingly neat inside for a long-term bachelor's residence. The only chairs were at a small kitchen table.

'Take a seat, Tom, and tell me what's on your mind while I make us some coffee. Sorry there's nothing stronger at present.'

'Coffee's fine for me, George. There's a young woman I know who is looking for a horse and I thought you might have one for sale. She can ride but I don't want something that has too much energy for her. I wouldn't want her to get hurt.'

Roberts gave a knowing smile.

'Sounds like the Pages' girl – Kitty, isn't it? I heard

you and her were fighting Indians together recently.'

'You're right. It's hard to keep secrets from you. How do you know so much?'

'A lot of folks call in here on their way back to their homes and ranches after trips to town. They all seem to feel sorry for a lonely old-timer like me and they drop in for a while. They keep me fairly well-informed. But about that horse – I have one that could be just what you want. She's a three-year-old black filly about fourteen hands; she's by my Morgan horse from a mustang mare.

'If she was a hand higher and a hundred or so pounds heavier I could name my own price for her. Trouble is, she's a bit small for a cow pony, wouldn't have the weight to hold a big steer on a rope. She's a good-looker, quiet but lively like a good horse should be.'

'Sounds like she could be what I want. If it suits you I'd like to have a look at her later, but now there's another thing I want to ask you about.'

'Go ahead.'

'I am looking for a man. I don't know his name. He might have some information I need.'

'Local gossip says you and the gunfighter Durango are looking for Ollie Harker. Is it something to do with that?'

'Might be,' Parry admitted. 'I'm not really sure but I don't want word of this to get about.'

'It won't. Folks tell me a lot but I am mighty careful what I tell others. What do you want to know?'

'This might sound odd, but I'm looking for a man

73

with a beard with a battered old hat turned up in front. Could be it's pinned up with a horseshoe nail.'

'I think I know who you mean. There ain't a lot of men with nails in their hats. There's a character named Crane who turns up in town occasionally. About two years ago he tried to sell me a couple of horses that had altered brands and were obviously stolen. I told him where to go and we don't exactly keep close company.

'He don't come to town much and folks say when he does, he spends most of his time at Monson's saloon. Nobody seems to know what he does for a living; just comes to town sometimes with a wagon, buys a few supplies and disappears again for weeks on end.'

'Would he know Ollie Harker?'

'I doubt it. Harker would be a bit too honest for his liking, and given that Ollie is away a lot the chances are that they have never met.'

'So you don't think there's any connection between Cookson's wagon and driver disappearing and this Crane character?'

'Cookson made his money by employing good men to manage his enterprises. Joe Murchison and Ollie Harker were both very smart men and his wagon drivers are the best. He would not have much use for someone like Crane. Now, let's go out and see that pony I told you about.'

Several horses were grazing in a small pasture behind the ranch house. One was a black pony, shining with good health. As it looked curiously towards the two men Parry saw that it had a white diamond on its forehead and two white hind fetlocks. The animal's conformation was superb; only its lack of size went against it as a cow pony. He had no doubt that under a light weight the pony would have both speed and stamina.

'She looks good to me, George. What price do you have on her?'

Roberts looked at the pony for a while.

'She's too small to breed the type of horse that I want and she's only eating valuable grass here,' he said quietly. 'I would like her to go to someone who would appreciate her. How does eight dollars sound?'

'I won't argue with that, George, but I'll have to see what Kitty thinks. What if I bring her up to see the pony?'

'Suits me. Bring her any time. She can take the pony back with her and try her out. If she's satisfied, she can pay me later, or if she don't like it she can send it back. But there's another thing. You haven't asked me so I reckon you don't know about the wagon.'

'What wagon?'

Roberts looked pensive, as though in doubt about pursuing the subject, but after a short pause he continued:

'I can't say this happened to me because this house is a mile away from the road, but a couple of my neighbours have mentioned hearing a wagon on the road very late at night or early in the morning. I know that road links us with the Overland Trail but honest folks don't travel at that hour.'

'Does this happen often?'

'I don't rightly know, but a couple of different

people have mentioned it to me. It has happened often enough to catch folks' attention. Could be there's some monkey business going on, in or near Logjam Creek, but that's all I know.'

Parry glanced at the sun and calculated he had about an hour before it set.

'Time I was on my way, George. Thanks for the help. If Kitty wants that pony I'll bring her out to see it.'

As he rode away Parry was feeling pleased with the horse deal, but he was still uncertain whether Crane had any connection with Harker's disappearance. His mind kept returning to the story of the mystery wagon. He recalled being told that someone had reported hearing a wagon around the time that Ewart was murdered.

Durango and Murchison had been detailed to follow up Harker's disappearance, so he would pass on the information.

Modoc Willie was wondering why Monson wanted him so urgently. Mentally he rehearsed the concocted excuse for the destruction of the still. He was not reassured by the saloon owner's smile because he knew that it was usually a false indication of what was really on his mind, but, much to his relief, the new task laid out for him was relatively simple.

Monson produced a large envelope from his desk drawer. He looked inside and withdrew a crumpled piece of paper on which was written one of the main parts of his plan. He studied it briefly, nodded in satisfaction and passed it to the half-breed. Then he carefully explained his plan.

It was simple but had to be done properly. If it worked, those hunting for Harker would be steered on to a false trail: one that led away from his own operations.

Willie had slipped into town unnoticed and turned over his hard-ridden horse to the alcoholic former cowboy who now cared for the horses of Monson and his men. Drunk or sober, Pete Cantwell was still very good with horses.

The interview with Monson had been short and Willie emerged into the afternoon light with twenty dollars in his pocket and a firm idea of what he had to do to earn it.

Cantwell had transferred his saddle to another horse and the Henry repeater was still slung to it. Without a word to the wrangler Willie mounted and steered the animal to the brush-covered hill just behind the town. Keeping under cover he ascended the slope until he found a suitable vantage point on the crest. He hitched the horse to a stunted tree on the reverse slope, took his rifle and carefully peered over the ridge's crest.

The back of Cookson's two-storey house was in easy rifle range and Willie could plainly see the two windows that were in the wall of the office. Both were open and gave enough light to see some details of the room. Even as he watched he saw movement, then Cookson's figure became visible as he passed the window.

Satisfied that his task would not be too demanding

the half-breed took the crumpled piece of paper from his pocket and looked for a place to leave it. He had to be careful that it did not blow away, but at the same time the paper must not look as though it had been planted.

A greasewood bush caught his eye; it proved ideal for the purpose. Tucked in among the low-growing branches, the paper was secure and plainly visible, as though it had been carried there by the wind.

Willie's next task was to position himself for a clear shot through the open window which, he had been told, was near Cookson's desk. Lying in a patch of weeds on the ridge crest, he checked his rifle sights and waited for his target to appear. As he watched he saw a middle-aged woman, whom he guessed to be Cookson's housekeeper. She had a basket and was making her way to a small garden not far from the back door. Here was his opportunity.

Willie fired. The bullet kicked up dirt at the woman's feet. She screamed, dropped the basket and fled into the house. Quickly he levered another cartridge into the firing chamber and moved his rifle to cover the open window. He was just in time, for Cookson looked out to see what was happening. Framed by the window he was an easy target, A squeeze of the trigger sent the bullet on its way. The heavy slug hit its intended mark.

Cookson reeled away from the window. His hand had been resting on the sill and he felt the jolt as the bullet buried itself in the wood only inches from his fingers. A second later another bullet came through the window and hit the wall on the opposite side of the room.

Boots clattered on the stairs, then Willie heard Murchison call:

'Are you all right, J.B.?'

'I am. Don't come in, Joe. The sonofabitch is shooting through the windows. Send someone to get Durango.'

His task accomplished, Modoc Willie ran back to his horse, jumped into the saddle and urged it down the back slope of the ridge. He figured that he had only a short period before Cookson's men came after him; it would be best if he was not observed.

Parry was deep in thought when he heard the galloping horse. *Someone in a hell of a hurry,* he told himself.

A rider came into view round a bend in the trail: a small man on a lanky bay horse. He flew past Parry with scarcely a glance as the latter was closing the front gate to Roberts's ranch. The rider's face, low over his mount's neck, was partly obscured by the horse's long mane but shoulder-length black hair streaming from beneath his hat branded him as an Indian or possibly a half-breed.

Parry sat on his horse and watched the rider, who was now somewhat obscured by the dust rising in his wake. Eventually another bend in the trail hid man and horse from view. Parry's first thought was that the stranger was up to no good; however, not being a law officer he would have no right to detain the man even if he managed to catch him.

'If I was a gambling man,' he said to his horse, 'I'd bet that that *hombre* has either stolen that horse or is running from something that has happened in town.'

NINE

Cookson's building was a hive of activity when Parry dismounted and hitched his horse to the rail in front of it. Several horses were already there, Durango's black being prominent among them.

Joe Murchison was talking to one of the office staff on the veranda; a hum of voices came from inside the building.

'Where the hell have you been?' The wagon master's greeting was hardly cordial.

'I've been asking around a few folks. What's happening?'

'Ollie Harker just tried to kill J.B.. Took a shot at him through one of the back windows – damn near got him, too.'

'Are you sure it was Harker? Did anyone see him?'

'Didn't need to see him. He accidentally dropped a receipt made out to him. Who else would it be?'

'As I was coming back to town a rider passed me. He was in a mighty big hurry. I couldn't get a good look at him but he could have been an Indian or a half-breed.

He had long black hair and was riding a big bay horse. How long is it since Cookson was shot at?'

'Maybe about an hour ago. Durango found where the shot came from. There were a couple of .44 rimfire shells and the receipt was caught up in a nearby bush. Looks like the shooter dropped it but didn't know. J.B. thinks that Harker has turned on him but can't figure out why.'

Parry was quick to admit that he had the same problem. If Harker had disappeared with Cookson's money it made little sense that he should go on a killing spree rather than enjoying his ill-gotten gains elsewhere. What old scores was he trying to settle?

Murchison admitted that he had similar doubts but had to consider the possibility that Harker had gone loco.

'What happens now?' Parry asked.

'Durango's taking out a few men to see if they can pick up the shooter's tracks. J.B. is really mad. He wants whoever it was to be caught as quick as possible.'

Parry could see little sense in that course of action.

'Durango is a good man to have in a fight but he couldn't track an elephant in snow,' he reasoned. 'In a few minutes it will be dark, so the chances of him finding something are mighty slim.'

Murchison disagreed.

'He has a good description of Harker and will know him if he runs across him.'

'Maybe, but the odds are that Harker is dead.'

Parry saw no point in riding out with Durango's party. Instead he attended to his horse and then walked to the Pages' house. Kitty saw him coming and was waiting at the gate. He hoped that the smile he saw on her face was more about him than eager anticipation of his news about a new horse. When he told her about the black pony her eyes lit up and the smile became broader. She ushered him through the gate and took his arm as though she was frightened he would escape.

'I have discussed this with my parents,' she told him. 'They are prepared to go to ten dollars for the right sort of pony. I don't suppose I can buy much for that.'

'I can get you a very good one for eight dollars if you like it.'

Parry was enjoying the role of being a bearer of good news. He proceeded to tell her about the pony and it pleased him to see her growing enthusiasm.

Mary Page, when told of the intention, was cautious at first. She wanted to be sure that her daughter was not buying some half-broken mustang that could injure her. Parry assured her that Kitty would be able to try the pony in a safe environment and that Roberts would not sell her a horse she could not handle. Knowing that Sandy would approve, Mary conditionally gave her consent.

It was agreed that Kitty would be ready with her sorrel pony at daybreak. Parry would meet her and they would ride to see the one that Roberts had. If she liked it they would bring it back to Logjam Creek and would be there by mid-morning, just in case Cookson needed Parry later in the day.

Kitty was ready and waiting astride her old pony when Parry arrived. She greeted him cheerfully as she turned her mount beside the roan, bombarding its rider with questions about the black pony that she had thought of after their previous meeting.

Parry was able to give positive answers to most of them and he knew that the ride would be an enjoyable one. For a while he would forget about the hunt for Harker. He had not slept well, troubled by thoughts about the mysterious rider he had seen.

Instinct told him that the man had something to do with the attempt to kill Cookson, but he had been told that the shooter had used a Henry or Winchester repeater. He had seen no sign of a rifle. Then he remembered that he had seen only the off side of the galloping horse. He could not have seen a weapon if it had been slung on the horse's other side.

It was inevitable that the conversation should turn to the recent shooting and Kitty expressed an idea about the rider he had seen. She asked if anyone had considered the possibility that the rider was a decoy intended to draw attention away from someone in town.

Parry had already discarded the theory about a stolen horse. Logjam Creek was a small town and the word would spread quickly if a horse was stolen. If the rider was in any way connected to the attempted shooting he must also have some connection to the missing wagon driver. The receipt could divert attention to Harker but, in his own mind, Parry was convinced that Harker was dead. Who stood to gain by such a deception?

Then there was the matter of Ewart's dying message. By some accounts he had just gasped Harker's name but others said the word had been '*Harker's*'. If the latter version was correct it could be a warning that the missing man might have been intending to do something – or that Ewart had seen something – that connected him to Harker. The most common theory was that Ewart was trying to name his killer.

He pushed his doubts to the back of his mind, determined not to let them spoil what he wanted to be a pleasant ride.

'You look worried, Tom.' Kitty had noticed his frown.

'Nothing serious. We are nearly at George's place. His front gate is round the next bend in the trail. Remember, if there's something about that pony that you don't like you don't have to buy it.'

Roberts had the black pony in the corral when they arrived. The introduction was brief and all three headed for the corral. Roberts smiled slightly when he saw the delighted look on Kitty's face.

'She's lovely, Mr Roberts. Does she have a name?'

'I just call her "Duchess" but anyone who buys her can call her what they want. Do you want to try her out?'

'Oh yes.'

'Come into the corral with me and you can get to know her. Tom will get your bridle and saddle off your other pony. She has not seen a woman before so it's best that you ride her in the corral till she gets used to you. She is a quiet pony but this is a new situation for her so it pays to be careful.'

Much to the watchers' relief, the little mare made no

objections to her new rider. Obediently she walked, trotted and cantered around the corral, stopped, and turned to a light touch on the reins. Kitty was delighted and, after a good try-out, announced that she would buy the pony and ride her home. Parry volunteered to lead the old sorrel.

'You have a good one there,' Roberts assured Kitty as they were leaving. 'Her mother was an Indian mustang, that's why she's a bit small for a man, but with a light-weight like you she could gallop all day if she was needed to. Just like people, horses miss their friends so she might be a bit upset for a couple of days. The quicker you become her best friend, the easier the change will be for her.'

Kitty patted the glossy black neck and laughed.

'I'll enjoy doing that.'

Parry felt strangely jealous and wondered if the new pony would take up too much of the time he was hoping to spend with Kitty.

Things had gone wrong for Modoc Willie during the night and disaster struck on top of the range, about halfway between the town and the moonshiners' camp. The old Indian trail was hard enough to follow in day-light as it twisted and turned among the trees and boulders. On such a dark night it took all the half-breed's skill to stay on course. The horse he rode had plenty of speed but was unused to rough country. Even at a slow walk it had stumbled on the uneven ground when he took it off the made road.

Then, on a steep section of the trail, it had slipped.

As it fell the rider was thrown head first against a tree trunk that had been invisible in the forest darkness. Unconscious, he slid twenty feet down the steep slope before being brought to a stop by another tree.

Regaining his senses, he had trouble at first comprehending what had happened. Then gradually he became aware of his situation. He was entangled in his one-ear bridle and guessed that he had somehow dragged it off the horse's head when he fell.

Of his mount there was no sign. Freed from the bridle it had wandered off, leaving him with a bad headache and a long walk to the camp. The animal would probably make its way back to where it considered its home to be. If it returned to Logjam Creek there was some chance that he might get back his saddle and rifle and Monson would know that something had happened to him.

For now, though, Willie had no choice. He had to continue his journey on foot and it would take several hours of hard walking.

Kitty and Parry sighted the bay horse trotting ahead of them when they rounded a bend in the trail. Even at a distance they could see the dirt smeared on the saddle and the animal's side, The lack of a rider and a bridle told a not uncommon story.

'Looks like someone's had an accident,' Parry observed. 'That horse passed me near here yesterday, going in the opposite direction. The rider was in a big hurry.'

'Do you think the man might be hurt somewhere?'

Kitty asked in a concerned voice.

'There's a good chance. We are nearly home, so I'll get you back to your place and then back-track that horse.'

'I could go on alone,' Kitty volunteered. Parry shook his head.

'Your pony has never seen a town and she might get spooked. If she does and you are leading your other horse you could have an accident. I want to be sure you get home safely.

'I'm also a bit curious to see what that horse does when it gets to town,' he added.

Ten minutes later, as they reached the Pages' house, they saw the bay horse turn and trot down the lane leading to the back of the saloon.

TEN

With Kitty safely home, Parry wasted no time. The bay horse had not reappeared from the lane, which suggested to him that the animal belonged to someone connected to the saloon. Local gossip was that Monson owned a couple of racehorses but Parry had not seen them. Certainly the horse and the tracks it left were larger than those of the usual cow ponies.

Murchison was in his downstairs office and listened in silence while Parry recounted the story of the riderless horse. The older man was not in favour of Parry going searching for the missing rider alone and suggested he should wait until Durango and his small posse arrived back in town. They would be tired and some of the men might need fresh horses. He also expressed the notion that the missing man could be Monsoon's responsibility. Parry did not agree with him.

'If that *hombre* was hurt coning off his horse he could be lying somewhere in a bad way. Time is important. My idea is to back-track that horse. If I find that the horse left the main trail I'll leave a small heap of stones to show I have turned to follow it. Also, I'll leave a plain trail for anyone to follow.'

'Suit yourself,' Murchison said. 'I'll tell Durango when he arrives but there's no guarantee that he will follow you straight away. Cookson might not agree with this idea.'

'He should, because I reckon this character could be the one who shot at him.'

'He might take a bit of convincing about that. He's sure that Harker was behind that try. That receipt was for a keg of Tabur's Special.'

'Never heard of it. What is it?'

'It's J.B.'s favourite beer. Most other beer doesn't travel very well in barrels over long distances but there's a fella named Tabur – runs a small brewery in Denver – and his beer keeps for weeks. Harker was supposed to pick up a keg and the receipt shows that he did, but I'm danged if I know where it is now.'

Parry walked to his horse.

'I have to get going at daybreak, Joe,' he said over his shoulder as he went. 'I'll try to get a bit of grub from Hendrick's bakery if it is open as I pass it. Could be a while before I get a chance to eat again. Durango might want to follow.'

'I wouldn't count on it,' Murchison told him.

The rest of the night was sure to be uncomfortable for Modoc Willie. His head ached and his right knee had become sore and swollen. Travelling in such condition on a dark night would be slow and dangerous. Reluctantly, he decided to settle down where he was until morning, when it would be easier to keep on the faint trail. Slowly and painfully he moved around, gathering a few dry twigs which he arranged to make the foundation of a fire. This task completed, he fished the makings from a pocket in his shirt and rolled a cigarette for himself.

For a while he rested and smoked. Then, never one to waste matches, he applied the smouldering cigarette butt to the twigs and fanned it with his hat. Seconds later a small flame burst into life. Limping about, he gathered some larger fallen branches which he added to the fire, making sure there was enough fuel to burn for several hours. Satisfied with his efforts he moved as close to the fire as he dared and stretched out to sleep.

At dawn Willie struggled to his feet and looked around for a suitable tree that would furnish a makeshift crutch. It took him a while to find one he could use. Even using his sharp Bowie knife it took him another half-hour to trim the branch to his satisfaction. By the time he was ready to move the horse he had lost had found its way to the Logjam Creek road.

Parry had little difficulty in tracking the bay horse back along the road as only he and Kitty had been over it since the previous day The hoofprints were large and clear in the soft dust and he could travel at a canter while following them.

Then, on a rocky section of the road, the tracks suddenly disappeared. Parry halted and looked about. On the eastern edge of the road he could see where the iron horseshoes had chipped some of the softer stones.

Further away from that spot he noticed a few twisted branches and disturbed leaves, indicating that the horse had come out of the close-growing timber on the mountainside. Once he was among the trees the hoof-prints were plainly visible on the softer ground. They meandered considerably because a loose horse would walk around obstacles that a rider might force a way through.

Another few minutes' back-tracking led to a faint trail that Parry knew would lead him over the mountains to where they had found the moonshiners' camp. Once on the trail he could make better time, although it was easy to miss in some places where the horse tracks did not show up.

In the hope that someone might follow him Parry built small pyramids of stones to indicate the direction he had taken. In other places he took his pocket knife and cut blazes on tree trunks, or cut off small green branches to drop along the trail. Anyone following would have an easy task. Meanwhile, he read what he could from the hoofprints.

The dry edges of some of the prints indicated that they had been made several hours before and he could only guess that the man he sought was some distance ahead. If he was healthy his man could be miles ahead, but if he was injured he could be around the next bend in the trail.

It was mid-afternoon before he found the spot where the horse had fallen, indicated by some low-growing bushes that had been trampled as it struggled to its feet. Near by were the ashes of a fire and some wood shavings. The ashes were still slightly warm but they showed that the injured man had several hours' start.

'Aubrey,' he said to his horse, 'we need to move a bit quicker if we want to find this *hombre* before dark.'

Modoc Willie heaved a sigh of relief as at last he descended the mountain range and reached the valley floor. He was now only about a mile from the camp. Already the mountain shadows were moving across the landscape and the sun was setting behind the crest of the western mountains. The light was fading quickly, so was Willie's strength. His injured knee was very painful and the improvised crutch had made his armpit sore. He calculated that he was about a mile from his companions at the sod hut.

He was reclining in the grass, having a short rest, when he glanced along his back trail and saw movement in the trees on the lower slope. Someone was on his trail. In a couple of moments, the rider would be clear of the trees and he had no chance of outrunning a horse. Then it occurred to him that if the horseman was alone he could ambush him and steal his horse. If there were more than one man trailing him he would lie low and allow them to pass. Keeping close to the ground, he rolled into a patch of long grass and found a shallow ditch where he could conceal himself until he had weighed the odds against him.

Parry rode out into the open. He recognized the area and knew where the injured man was heading. He could see no one ahead and, uncertain about how long a start the man had had, he assumed that he would already have reached the moonshiners' camp.

'One thing's sure,' he said to his horse, 'there's some connection between Monson and this bunch, and the receipt the shooter left behind ties him to Harker. Aubrey, old friend, there are more players in this game than anyone thought.'

Modoc Willie peered through a concealing tuft of grass and recognized the rider on the roan horse. When he saw that Parry was alone he decided that if the stranger ventured into pistol range he could ambush him; with luck he could also capture the horse.

Keeping movement to a minimum in case it attracted attention, he slowly eased his big Remington revolver from its holster and crouched lower in the grass.

Parry's course was straight up a clear grassy flat about a quarter of a mile wide. The mountains were on his left, rolling wooded hills were on his right. The absence of smoke confirmed that the moonshiners' still had not been repaired. But he knew that he was close to the camp and danger could be expected from the right side of the valley. With that in mind he kept to the middle of the open ground, hoping that the moonshiners did not have a sentry posted in the trees.

The need for tracking was over. Parry let his eyes stray from the ground immediately in front of him. Only when the roan horse snorted nervously did his attention return to his immediate surroundings. A few yards ahead he could see what looked like a broken tree branch on the ground. Then he saw the fresh knife cuts on the wood and realized that it was the crutch that the injured man had improvised.

Modoc Willie suddenly surged out of the long grass to Parry's left, holding a big revolver at arm's length before him.

Parry urged his horse with the spurs and it bounded ahead. Simultaneously the moonshiner fired. What should have been a killing shot was spoiled as the shooter's injured knee gave way.

Even then the bullet buzzed past Parry's ear as he concentrated upon putting distance between himself and the gunman. Two strides more and the roan horse had carried him out of pistol range. When another shot missed by a wider margin it was clear that the would-be assassin had missed both his target and his best chance.

For safety's sake Parry increased the gap by about another fifty yards before reining in his horse and slipping from his saddle. As he dismounted he snatched his Winchester carbine from its scabbard. But when he looked back to see his attacker it was as if the man had never existed. The landscape revealed no sign of another human being. Modoc Willie had gone to ground.

Weighing the odds against a lucky hit from the Indian's pistol, Parry stood on a small rock to get a better view. He could plainly see the attempted ambush site and could trace the shallow depression in which the attacker had hidden, but at first he saw no sign of the man himself. One large clump of long grass and weeds appeared to be the only spot where the shooter could be hiding, so he fired a couple of shots aimed close together in the hope of hitting his man or forcing him to move.

His target had stretched himself full length against a small bank, barely a foot high, which was screened by grass and weeds. Parry's shots cut through the long grass above him, missing him by only the barest of margins. It took steady nerves to remain still as a couple more bullets passed so close that he felt the draught, but Willie knew that it would be fatal to betray his position. His best chance was that Parry would become over-confident and stray into pistol range.

Bonner and Crane had finished loading the wagon and were about to harness the mules when they heard the shooting.

'I don't like the sound of that,' Crane said. 'Put a bridle on a couple of mules while I get our rifles from the soddy. That could be Willie in trouble. I was wondering what was keeping that little sonofabitch.'

Bonner was more cautious. 'Don't go rushing into things. We need to keep in the trees till we see what's going on.'

'I know that, you jackass. We need to spy things out a bit but the sooner we get there the quicker we'll know which side to take.'

ELEVEN

Modoc Willie had good reason to be worried. He knew from the angle of the incoming bullets that Parry was moving about, seeking a place where he could see into his refuge. So far the tall grass had screened him but it would not stop a bullet. Sooner or later Parry would find a position of advantage and when that happened his revolver would prove inferior to his enemy's Winchester. There was a chance that his fellow moonshiners would hear the shooting and come to investigate, but the men felt little loyalty to each other. It was also possible that they had taken flight at the sounds of the first shots.

Parry was regretting his decision to dismount. Though it made for more accurate shooting the extra elevation would have allowed a better view of his surroundings The shooter had not fired since the failure of the ambush and he had seen no movement from where the man had taken refuge. Possibly one of his rifle bullets had found its mark: he could be hunting a man seriously wounded or already dead.

His horse was standing, reins down, about a hundred yards away and he began backing towards it while keeping an eye on where his attacker probably lay. He risked a quick glance over his shoulder to make sure he was taking the shortest route. Just in time he saw the roan lift its head and look towards the trees where, Parry knew, the moonshiners' camp was concealed.

Then his attention was suddenly diverted from Modoc Willie as Parry heard breaking twigs and the sound of heavy animals forcing their way through the closely growing trees.

Glancing over his shoulder he saw two men on mules emerging through the screen of foliage. Both had rifles and they were between him and his horse. The nearer rider advertised his harmful intentions by throwing his rifle to his shoulder. Parry did likewise but Crane fired first.

Triggered from the back of a nervous mule, the shot was not only wasted but worked to the shooter's disadvantage. Unfamiliar with the sound of firearms in such close vicinity, the mule dropped its head and bucked. Riding bareback and taken completely by surprise, Crane was speared over the animal's head. He landed hard. He was stunned and groping blindly for the rifle he had dropped when Parry shot him.

Bonner was determined not to make the same mistake. He slid from his mule to hit the ground running. It took several strides before he regained his proper balance and turned to face his adversary. Parry was already swinging his Winchester towards him.

Modoc Willie now joined the fight. The long-range

pistol shot passed close enough to Parry to remind him that he was still between at least two determined shooters.

Crane was badly wounded. He had ceased trying to reach his rifle but his intended victim was within pistol range. He drew his six-shooter, propped himself up with both elbows and sought his target. With failing strength he struggled to cock the revolver; then, as he was fumbling, he accidentally fired the weapon.

The bullet went nowhere near Parry but it served to remind him that he was facing three men, all of whom were capable of shooting. He judged Bonner to be the most dangerous because he still had a rifle. A slight problem with the cartridge feeder had delayed his shooting but now the moonshiner was squinting along his sights. He was about to fire.

Parry brought his rifle to his shoulder and squeezed the trigger as soon as the front sight showed against the moonshiner's faded red shirt.

The impact of the bullet spun Bonner around and his unfired rifle fell from his hands. His most dangerous opponent now being out of the fight, Parry sought another target.

Muffled hoofbeats made him aware of a horseman racing to the scene. Though a white foam from hard riding covered much of its neck and shoulders, it was easy to recognize Durango's black. The gunman sat astride him, applying the spurs as he took aim with the revolver in his right hand.

Modoc Willie had been distracted by the fight with Parry and had not heard the horse on the soft grass until it was dangerously close. In alarm he twisted around but had no chance to shoot. Durango was within a couple of yards of him. Almost casually the rider fired one shot into Modoc as he flashed past; then, with his first target down, he steered his horse towards where Crane had struggled to a sitting position. He fired another shot and the moonshiner collapsed on to the ground.

Parry looked up from the corpse of Bonner as the black horse halted and stood with heaving sides a short distance away.

'Nice to see you. I was in deep trouble there for a while.'

'So I noticed,' Durango said as he dismounted. 'Old Midnight here has covered a lot of miles of late and we couldn't get here any quicker. Good to see you're not hurt. Let's see what we can find out about our dear departed friends. It will be dark soon.'

They dragged the three bodies together and Durango proceeded to search them. He instantly recognized Bonner.

'I know this murdering sonofabitch. His name is Wilf Bonner. He has a bad name as a treacherous skunk. Some say he's real sneaky and has killed a few men but the law has never been able to prove it. Story is that he is wanted in Texas but I'm not sure.'

As he removed the dead man's gunbelt Durango looked with disdain at the holstered revolver, which was rusted and looked badly neglected, indicating a dangerous carelessness for a man said to be a gunfighter. Then, inside the man's loose shirt, he found the small .32 revolver. It was clean and well cared-for.

'The sneaky coyote! The gun on his belt is only a decoy. The hideout gun is rigged for a left-handed draw. He would have been keeping his right hand away from the gun, where people could see it, while he drew this little gun left-handed. That coachbuilder, Ewart, was killed by a .32. The doc dug the slug out of him. The gun barrel had been so close to Ewart that the flash singed his shirt. This sonofabitch might be the one who shot Ewart.'

'Could be,' Parry agreed, 'but why? Most folks think it was Harker. His last words are supposed to have been something about Harker.'

'We can worry about that later. Let's see what we can find at the moonshiners' camp. For all we know there could be more of these no-goods waiting for us there. Until we know different, we need to tread very carefully here.'

With great caution the pair scouted the moonshiners' camp until they were reasonably certain that it was deserted. Then they set about examining the site before darkness fell. They found a loaded wagon and a couple of half-harnessed mules tethered near by.

There was a lantern in the shack. Durango volunteered to keep searching if Parry would round up the mules the dead men had been riding and bring them back to the camp. Parry also took along a sack to collect the personal effects and weapons that Durango had put to one side when they were examining the bodies. There was little of value among the few possessions but the guns could not be left in case they were found later by wandering Indians.

The mules were grazing quietly when Parry found them, having recovered from the recent excitement in which they had been briefly involved. They made no objection when Parry took their dangling reins and led them back to the camp. He left the guns in the sack near the dead men, finding it too awkward to carry while he was leading the mules.

Durango had been exploring and found the trail to the mule pasture. He helped Parry unharness the mules that the moonshiners had left tied to the wagon wheels; a short while later the two men placed their horses and the mules in the hidden enclosure, where they could find feed, water and, more important, rest. The horses had covered many miles in the last few days.

Weary and hungry though they were, neither man felt like sleeping in the sod hut, which to them had all the appeal of a pigsty. Instead, they rearranged the furs and skins in the wagon so that there was room for one man to sleep. The other would sit on the driver's seat and act as a guard. There was little chance of a man falling asleep on the hard wooden seat.

Using Durango's large, silver, stem-winder watch, they worked out a system of two-hour shifts. The pair had nothing to fear from the moonshiners but the shooting might have attracted the attention of a small group of Cheyennes. When pursued by the army, the Indians would disperse in small groups that often turned up in unlikely places.

Both men were glad to see daylight. After alternate bouts of broken sleep and uncomfortable sentry duty, neither felt rested and they were ravenously hungry. They planned to hitch up the wagon with the plunder from the camp and, with a light load and the mules fresh, they hoped to reach Logjam Creek that night.

'What about those dead men?' Parry asked. 'It don't seem right to leave them to the wolves and coyotes.'

'Those skunks would probably poison anything that tried to eat them but I suppose you're right. There's a hole been dug just behind the soddy. Looks like they were planning to bury something. There's a shovel there. If you harness the mules I'll dig that hole bigger and we can plant them before we leave. Maybe the law, such as it is, might be interested in digging them up some time later.'

'There could be a problem with the mules. We don't know which ones are the leaders for the team.'

'I'll leave you to figure that out,' Durango growled. 'I never had much dealing with those dumb jackasses. I dislike digging holes but it beats fighting those critters.'

That arrangement suited Parry because he knew that mules' bad behaviour was often triggered by impatience or cruel handling. Those who had taken the trouble to learn their ways had found mules to be quite intelligent. To his mind, working with stock was better than digging holes any day of the week.

They collected their horses and the mules. After hitching the horses to nearby trees, Durango started digging while Parry sorted out the tangle of harness that had been dumped under the wagon. In contrast to most of the moonshiners' equipment, the harness was in good order.

Parry was a good hand with stock; talking quietly and moving deliberately he had the mules standing calmly while he harnessed them. The usual system was to select the two tallest animals as leaders; fortunately, when he'd done that and harnessed them, the mules moved unbidden to the sides where they normally worked. The wheel pair were slightly smaller but heavier and the breeching marks on their ungroomed hindquarters confirmed their places in the team.

Durango had raised a good sweat by the time Parry announced that the wagon was ready. Thankfully he laid aside the shovel, wiped his forehead on his sleeve and climbed up beside Parry.

'That hole will have to do,' he announced. 'It's long enough and wide enough. It could be a lot deeper but I don't reckon the dear departed will worry. We can put a few rocks on top to stop any critters digging down.'

They collected the bodies and the sack of weapons and personal effects. Halting as close to the hole as they could get, they removed the tattered wagon canopy and used it to line the hole. With the three bodies in place they folded the overlap of the canvas on top of them and filled in the hole. They would not saddle their horses but would hitch them to the tail of the wagon to give them a rest after days of hard usage.

As he fastened his horse Durango saw the wagon for the first time in daylight.

'With that rotten canopy gone you can see there's a good, strong wagon under the dirt. I wonder where those coyotes stole it?'

A second later, quite by chance, Parry found the answer to that question.

TWELVE

'This is Harker's wagon. I couldn't recognize it with the canvas on but look at the back of the seat.'

Durango glanced in the direction Parry indicated and saw a small brass plate attached to the seat back. It read:

H. EWART
COACH MAKER
DENVER.

It was well-known that Cookson had enticed the Denver coachbuilder to Logjam Creek to keep his fleet of freight wagons maintained.

'I reckon those moonshiners had some sort of trouble with their old wagon and decided to steal Harker's,' Parry continued. 'They dirtied it up a bit and put an old canopy on it. Then they burned the old one to make it look like the Indians had killed Harker, so Cookson would have stopped looking for the missing wagon.'

'What happened to Harker?'

'I'm pretty sure he's dead. His body could have been dumped anywhere out here. Maybe, in years to come, someone might find a few bones scattered about after the buzzards and wolves were finished with his remains.'

'That makes sense,' Durango agreed. 'But where does Ewart fit into this?'

'By all accounts his dying words were something about Harker. Folks thought he was trying to say that Harker had killed him. I think he was trying to say that he had seen Harker's wagon. You said yourself that Bonner could have killed Ewart. My guess is that Bonner took the wagon to town early one morning without knowing that Ewart had built it. Ewart recognized the missing wagon and Bonner killed him.'

'Makes sense – but why would he take a wagon to town so early in the morning when no shops were open?'

Parry pointed to two boxes of bottles near the wagon.

'He was picking up a load of empty bottles from Monson's saloon.'

'That's right. Someone in town told Murchison that they heard an old wagon rattling along the street. They didn't hear the shot or see the wagon but sure as hell someone heard it. Those bottles would have been clinking and the boxes knocking together. A few of the bottles might have been broken. There's still a lot of broken glass over there near where the wagon was parked.'

'Looks like we can at least tell Cookson that we have found his wagon, solved the mystery of who shot Ewart and give him a fair indication as to what happened to Harker. Durango, you and I might soon be out of work again.'

'Don't celebrate too soon, young fella. Cookson's money is still missing and there's the little matter of someone trying to let daylight into him. Looks like it was that Indian moonshiner – but why?'

'Danged if I know,' Parry admitted. 'Maybe he fired someone who held a grudge, or it could be that a business rival planned the whole thing.'

Durango frowned and shook his head.

'He had no rival in these parts. More likely someone found out that Harker was carrying money and wanted to stop Cookson from searching for it. If that was the case I can see where those moonshiners were involved.'

'They were mixed up with this business but, by the look of them, they didn't have the money that Harker was carrying. The Indian knew something about Harker, certainly enough to plant that receipt that he could only have got from Harker.'

'All this thinking is giving me a headache, Tom. But there's one thing I know for sure, you and I have shot all the people who could have supplied the answers. With hindsight, that might not have been a good idea.'

'I don't see that we had a lot of choice there. I'm not a good enough shot to shoot just to wound.'

'Nor am I. The secret of my trade, if you could call it that, is to hit 'em in the biggest part first and do any fancy shooting only when you are sure they can't shoot back. It's a trade that you should avoid taking up, Tom. No matter how good you are, there's always someone better. You might never meet him but he could be behind the next bend in the road. If I think about this too much I'm inclined to get drunk and that's dangerous for a man like me.'

Monson strolled out on to the balcony where Al Webber was sitting in the shadows, his presence betrayed only by the red spark of his cigarette.

'No sign of anyone, Al?'

'Not a sign. I reckon something's gone wrong. Them moonshiners were to send word as soon as they had cleared out the camp. They've had enough time.'

'With Parry and later Finch on Willie's trail, there's a good chance they caught up with him before he reached the camp. We know he lost his horse. Damnit, Al! Things could go to hell real quick if one of those moonshiners has talked. I'm beginning to think, too, that they might also have double-crossed me. They sent in about four hundred dollars in stolen cash that the Indians traded for whiskey, but that's nothing compared to the payroll money that Harker was carrying for Cookson.'

Webber had heard the saloon gossip but he knew that such information was often wrong.

'I heard that story but I don't think Crane and the others would dare double-cross you. They ain't real smart but they know that you would hunt them down if they started playing games.'

'Round up a few of the boys, Al. I want one to ride

109

out to the moonshiners' camp and find out what's going on. We want someone with a few brains this time. He's to get back here as soon as he knows what's happened. Get a couple of reliable hardcases, because this business might end in shooting if Cookson finds out our involvement.'

Webber stood up and thought for a second or two.

'I can get young Pete Keller to ride out to the camp and find out what's been going on. He's a smart young rooster. Artie Small and Bill Lindsay are lying low a couple of miles from here after a serious brush with the law in Kansas. Keller can give your message to them as he passes their shack. They are two mighty tough customers who don't mind hiring out their guns. I don't think Cookson can recruit too many like them in a hurry.'

'What about Finch?'

'He's overrated and he's gettin' old and nervous. I can handle him.'

'How good is that young Parry who hangs around with Finch?'

'From what I hear he's had a few Indian fights,' Webber said dismissively. 'But that ain't like fighting white men at close range. There's a hell of a difference between shooting men at long range with a rifle and facing a white gunman with a six-shooter at close range. He won't be much of a problem.'

Pete Keller was tall and thin; it was claimed that he had to stand in the one place twice to make a shadow. He had been a good cowhand until he succumbed to the lure of the crooked dollar. As a road agent his single-handed coach robberies had been meticulously planned and he had always been smart enough to move to new territory before the law could identify him. Somewhere in his travels he had fallen in with Al Webber and now he lived quietly, picking up the odd dishonest dollar without attracting attention.

An hour after receiving instructions he rode out of Logjam Creek. Another hour later he stopped at the hideout of Small and Lindsay and passed on Monson's offer. Both had been drinking heavily the night before and Keller had trouble waking them, but he made sure that they understood his message. Then he mounted his horse and set off at a smart pace for the moonshiners' camp.

He left the main trail for the short cut over the mountains and halted at the first line of ridges to rest his horse for a few minutes. From the crest of the ridge he could see part of the road some miles away on the western side of the range. As he watched, Keller saw a distant cloud of dust and a tiny dot that gradually became a single wagon.

Instinct told him that the sighting could be important; reluctantly he delayed his journey. Another fifteen or so minutes would not be noticed by people who were not expecting him.

Logjam Creek followed a winding course down the valley and the road had many twists in it. The wagon changed direction slightly and as it took one of the bends Keller had an almost side-on view. By then it was close enough for him to discern a couple of horses being led behind the vehicle: a black and a red roan.

He knew who owned these animals and the sun glinting off Durango's silver-studded hatband confirmed his suspicions. He decided not to go to his intended destination, reasoning that Monson would be more concerned that the stolen wagon was coming to town.

Hastily he retraced his steps, recklessly urging his mount down the steep slopes. He preferred not to be seen and he had to reach the road before the wagon came along.

But he was seen.

Kitty had been riding her new pony, exploring along the same road. The day was warm and she was being careful not to work Duchess too hard until the animal was in working condition. A loop of the creek was close to the road, so she found an easy place that allowed access to the stream. The pony saw and smelled the cool water and eagerly dipped her nose into it.

Then, almost immediately, she lifted her head again. With pricked ears she looked towards the wooded slope across the creek. Kitty heard it too: a heavy body moving quickly, smashing through undergrowth and the deadwood that littered the forest floor.

A hundred yards away a rider burst from the trees, splashed across the shallow creek and plunged up the steep bank to the road. He halted his mount briefly and, standing in his stirrups, he looked southwards down the trail for a second or two, as though searching for something.

Kitty glimpsed a very tall man who seemed to tower

over his horse. He paid no attention to anywhere but the road, so he never saw the young woman and her pony, who were partly obscured by a clump of willows on the creek bank. Something was seriously alarming the stranger; after a brief halt he turned his horse and galloped towards the town. He was out of sight by the time the young woman had allowed her pony a quick drink before returning to the road.

This time Duchess also looked to the south; her rider could hear approaching hoofs and the rattle of a wagon. Sound carried a long way in the stillness; Kitty's wait was longer than she expected but then a wagon with a four-mule team came round a bend in the road. To her surprise, she recognized Parry and Durango.

'Looks like we have a welcoming committee,' the gunman observed, glancing sideways at Parry. 'The way that girl's waving makes me think she's mighty glad to see us – or at least one of us. I wonder what she's doing out here?'

THIRTEEN

'She's just trying out her new pony.' Parry tried to sound casual.

'Shouldn't be out here alone, though. There's too many strange customers about, let alone Indian raiders who might have split up to avoid the army.'

Pleased to see Kitty, Parry forgot about the cautionary lecture that had first come to his mind. He steadied the team as they approached the young woman waiting by the road side.

'I didn't expect to meet you out here. How's Duchess going?'

'She's wonderful – everything I wanted in a pony. I didn't expect to meet you here, especially driving a wagon.'

'There's a long story behind this,' Durango explained, 'but we've found Cookson's missing wagon.'

'Unfortunately there's no sign of the missing driver,' Parry added.

'I don't know if it's important,' Kitty said, 'but just a while ago I saw a rider come out of the forest over there. He was in a big hurry. He was looking down the road for a while as though he might have been expecting to see you. He galloped off towards town just a short while before you came around the corner.'

'What did he look like?' Durango asked.

'He was tall and very thin and dressed like a cowhand. He had a sorrel horse and it looked like it had been working hard. It was covered in sweat.'

'I think I know the *hombre* you saw,' Durango told her. 'I've seen him at Monson's a time or two.'

'The trail over the mountains to the moonshiners' camp meets this road around about here, give or take a quarter-mile or so,' Parry said. He turned to Durango. 'Could be that he was checking on the situation and saw us from up on the hill. My guess is that he is riding hard to warn someone in Logjam Creek.'

Durango agreed. 'There's no prize for guessing who that might be. I reckon I'll leave you here and ride ahead to warn Cookson just in case someone is planning to bushwhack us.'

Parry turned to Kitty. 'I want you to go with Durango. He can escort you right to your door on his way to Cookson's outfit. I won't be far behind you with the wagon. There could be trouble, so when you get to town stay indoors until someone you know tells you it's safe to come out.'

'My pa works for Cookson. Is he likely to be involved in this?'

'Maybe, but go with Durango now because if your pa is involved somebody needs to be with your mother. I'll see you later in town.'

Durango had gladly left the wagon for the comfort of his saddle. He ranged his big horse beside Kitty's pony.

'Now, young lady,' he said, 'we will find out just how well that horse of yours can travel.'

Parry watched the pair depart, then transferred his Winchester from his saddle to the seat beside him. Like a pebble in a boot, one ominous notion kept coming into his mind and refused to be rationalized away. If the mysterious rider was a lookout man for an already arranged ambush Durango and Kitty were in mortal danger. If not, the riders could be ignored and the wagon left as the main target. He could only trust to luck. He urged the mules into a brisk trot, all the while listening for the burst of gunfire that would indicate that Kitty and Durango had struck trouble.

Keller did not spare his horse and did not care who saw him as he urged the weary animal down the street and turned it into the lane beside the saloon.

Webber had seen him coming and was looking over the balcony. As the rider dismounted, he called down to him:

'Pete – what's wrong?'

'Durango and Parry – they're headed this way and they've got a wagon. Better tell Monson. Ain't much time.'

'I'll see you in Monson's office,' Webber yelled. He had just seen Kitty and Durango gallop up to the Pages' house and halt there.

'Get your horse behind the house and get inside,'

Durango told Kitty urgently. 'And keep away from the front windows. This house is in range of any stray shots from the saloon.'

Half-expecting to be fired upon, Durango wheeled his mount and galloped for Cookson's freight depot, which was another hundred yards past Monson's establishment. Joe Murchison met him as he dismounted in front of the office.

'Where have you been?' he demanded.

'I'll explain later. Young Tom's coming in with Harker's wagon and Monson's crowd might try to stop him. Gather as many men with guns as you can and get them out here to cover Parry when he arrives. Monson's linked to Harker's disappearance. Start moving!'

Murchison was not used to being ordered about, but seeing the urgency on Durango's face he realized that argument would not help the situation. For the first time in several years he actually ran.

The first person he met was Cookson, who had heard the commotion and was hurrying down the stairs from his office. Before his boss could enquire, Murchison told him:

'Tom Parry is coming in with Harker's wagon. Monson's crew might try to stop him. We need men with guns to back up Durango.'

The town came in sight at last and Parry shouted at his weary team. They responded as though sensing that their long hard journey was about to end. With great relief he caught a glimpse of Kitty's pony at the back of

117

the house, but when he looked to the road again he saw Al Webber and another tall man moving out from the front of the saloon, as if to bar his way.

Then, looking beyond Monson's men, he saw Durango walk out into the street with his rifle in his hand.

Monson's men had been watching the approaching wagon until they heard Durango call. They turned to see him with his rifle to his shoulder, squarely aimed at Webber.

'Let that wagon through, Al,' he called. 'If one shot is fired, you're dead meat. You might not hit me at this distance with a six-gun but I sure as hell won't miss you with this rifle. The first shot I hear will be the last one you hear.'

Webber turned and saw that Durango was not making an empty threat. Behind the gunman he saw Cookson, Murchison, Hockley and the elder of the Harper boys fanning out across the street, each armed with a Winchester repeater.

'Let the wagon through, Pete,' he called. 'We're outnumbered here.'

Keller did not argue. He had reached the same conclusion. Both men walked back to the saloon veranda as a much-relieved Parry passed them in the wagon.

Durango backed away slowly. He knew that he had made a dangerous enemy. The problem would have to be settled one way or another before he left Logjam Creek.

FOURTEEN

Monson had been watching through the saloon's open door. Now he called his two gunmen into the building. He was realist enough to know that the odds were against him. Things would be different when Small and Lindsay arrived. He had forgotten about the store of repeating rifles that Cookson held in order to arm his employees at short notice.

Webber was fuming. He knew that he had been very close to death because Durango had not given him any chance to defend himself.

He informed his companions that he would never be caught in such a situation again.

Monson was more worried than angry. It was bad luck that the moonshiners had chosen to steal that particular wagon and so attract the attention of the Cookson outfit. The murder of Ewart had been too close to home. He had been careful to conceal his involvement in the whiskey-running operation but somehow it had become known.

He thought of the large envelope in his desk drawer,

which held the few personal items taken from Harker. Using the old receipt to divert attention on to the missing teamster had somehow failed. The idea had seemed good at the time but the envelope and its contents would now be damning evidence against him. It would have to be destroyed, but at present there were more pressing issues.

The extent of Cookson's knowledge greatly worried him He was almost sure that the moonshiners were dead but had any of them talked before they died? Rumours of a missing payroll were another complication. If the rumours were true and he had not been told about it there was a good chance that the whiskey-runners were not as loyal as he had thought.

Monson was a rich man. He did not intend to jeopardize his position by stealing money from someone as powerful as Cookson. Even with the fringe of law many miles away such a theft would eventually attract lawmen. The loss of a wagon and a teamster at a time when Indians were raiding could be explained: the wagon turning up with his men aboard was sure to generate many embarrassing questions.

Webber was pacing the balcony, trying to see what was happening at Cookson's and watching for his badly needed reinforcements. Trouble was coming and the gunman knew that Monson had too much at stake to leave all and run. He had promised himself that he would square accounts with Durango before he left Logjam Creek. He would seek a confrontation at the first opportunity; he had convinced himself that he would prevail. He was sure that Finch was getting older, slower and more nervous. Claiming his scalp would bring Webber into the world of high-priced hired guns.

Murchison and Cookson watched as Parry halted the wagon in front of them.

'Durango and I reckon this is probably Harker's wagon,' Parry told them. 'What do you think ?'

'That's it,' Cookson answered immediately. 'Ewart and I worked on designing a few modifications to this one. I'd know it anywhere. Where did you get it?'

Durango pointed to the mountains.

'A bunch of moonshiners over those mountains had it. They were trading whiskey to the Indians. You can see the furs and buffalo robes in the back.'

'Any sign of Harker?' Murchison demanded.

'Not a sign,' said Parry. 'We reckon he must be dead.'

Cookson walked over to the wagon and undid the hasp of the large grub box bolted to the side. He lifted the lid and looked into the box. It contained a battered coffee pot, a few cooking utensils and the remains of food that had long since turned mouldy. To protect the teamsters' supplies in bad weather and river crossings, the box's interior was lined with tin. Piece by piece Cookson emptied the box, throwing its contents in an untidy pile at the roadside. When it was empty, he studied the interior briefly.

'I need a screwdriver,' he told Murchison. 'I think I have sadly misjudged Ollie Harker.'

As he rummaged through the toolbox under the driver's seat the wagon boss complained.

'J.B., what are you talking about? Stop being so darn mysterious. Anyway, here's the screwdriver.'

'Look in here, Joe, and I'll show you what I'm talking about. See those two screws? Do you see those little red spots in the slots in the screwheads?'

'Sure. They look like little specks of paint.'

Cookson was enjoying the moment.

'They're not paint. That red stuff is sealing wax, put there by the bank. Any attempt to turn those screws would have dislodged the dabs of wax. They are a security measure.'

'Were you worried about someone stealing the lining of the grub box? Stop playing games with us, J.B.. What's going on?'

The screws were slightly rusted but eventually they turned and were loosened. Cookson lifted the tin liner of the box clear and dropped it with a clang that startled the mules. Luckily Parry still had a firm hold of the reins.

'That liner covered a false bottom. If you look in there, Joe, you will see a canvas-wrapped package with bank seals on it. That's the missing payroll. You should be happy to know that you will all be paid at the end of the month. I thought Harker might have been conspiring with someone to steal the money. I am glad to see that I was wrong.'

Durango shook his head in apparent disbelief.

'Do you mean to say that those dumb moonshiners thought they were only stealing a wagon because something had happened to the one they had?'

'Looks like it. I told Ollie that he was not to risk his

life trying to protect the money. He was free to hand it over if he was held up. My guess is that they killed him before he had a chance to bargain for his life.'

Murchison pushed his hat back from his forehead.

'How do you reckon Monson is involved in all this?'

'He's in it for sure,' Parry declared. 'He was supplying the empty bottles. Most whiskey-runners sell to the Indians from a barrel, a tin cup at a time, but by putting it in bottles they can get better deals from their customers. It is safer for those concerned because they can take their poison away and they don't congregate at the wagon or still.

'Army patrols are always chasing hostiles and things would go badly if they caught them and the moonshiners together. Folks have been talking for a while about hearing wagons on the road at strange hours. You can bet that what they heard was the moonshiners delivering loot to Monson or taking away a load of empty bottles.'

'Not only that,' Durango added. 'A moonshiner named Bonner almost certainly killed Ewart, the wagon builder. Ewart must have recognized the stolen wagon. Bonner wasn't from around these parts and didn't know that Ewart had built it.'

'Where's Bonner now?' Cookson asked.

Durango allowed himself a grim smile.

'Around about now I reckon he'd be in hell. Young Tom here shot him. I sent another coupla no-goods in the same direction.'

'Who were they?' Cookson asked.

'One was an Indian,' Durango told him. 'We think

he was the one who tried to shoot you. We don't know the other one. We kept some of their personal stuff in case the law was interested. It's in the wagon.'

'That's the bit I can't follow. Why did they want to kill me?'

'I'm only guessing, but with Harker missing and Ewart dead, the law is going to be here some day soon asking questions. They wouldn't look too closely at Monson if they thought Harker was alive and gunning for you and his former friend, Ewart.

'Seeing as how Harker knew about the payroll, he had a good motive to go bad. It wouldn't have mattered whether the shooter hit you or not. The idea that Harker was still alive was planted and no one would be interested in Monson.'

Murchison still had his doubts about the situation.

'Even if all this is true we might still have trouble tying Monson into all this. If it comes to a court case he'll have the best lawyer and the best jury that money can buy.'

'What about that receipt that had Harker's name on it?' Parry asked.

'We can't prove that Monson arranged for it to be found. There was no reason for him to have it. We can't even prove that the shooter had it.'

'We know that the Indian was riding one of Monson's racehorses,' Parry argued.

'Don't tell me that you, of all people, don't know that Indians steal horses,' Murchison replied with a snort like that of an angry bull. 'Monson only needs to say that the man was a horse thief.'

Cookson decided to close the discussion.

'Much as I would like to, we can't just go into Monson's place and start shooting,' he told them. 'Unless we have good evidence that Monson or his men are involved in these murders we have to wait for the law. It will be here eventually and we have to do things by the book. None of us want to be facing murder charges.

'However, if they attack us – meaning myself or any of my employees – we start shooting. I know there are a few of my people who are married and living in town. At the first sign of trouble I want these men to go home and make sure they have a good gun, but unless their families are in direct danger they are to stay out of things. Any others are free to quit now or fight later if they decide to stay.'

'I'll be staying,' Durango said. 'I'm kind of curious to see how this mess finally ends up.'

'You can count me in too,' Parry declared. He thought it best not to mention his reasons for staying.

FIFTEEN

Small and Lindsay arrived just before sundown. They knew better than to attract attention. To the casual observer they were just a pair of ranch hands who were headed for the saloon after a day's work. But a more curious onlooker would have noted that both men had carbines on their saddles; he might even have noticed that each of them had an extra revolver stuck in his belt.

Instead of hitching their horses to the rail in front of Monson's, they turned into the lane that led to the stables and corrals at the rear of the building. Webber saw them arrive. From the balcony he told them where to put their horses and saddles. Then he came downstairs to meet them.

'Is it all over or hasn't it started yet?' Small asked when Webber let them into the saloon by the rear door.

'So far nothing's happened, but Cookson's gathering his men and they're likely to come calling at any time.'

'What are the odds?' Lindsay wanted to know. He

126

was a man of few words but he did not like working with careless people. The more he knew about the other side the better were his chances of survival.

Webber did not mince words.

'I reckon Cookson has the numbers but they're mostly wagon drivers. They can all shoot but he only has one first-class gunman, Durango Finch.'

'How many more does he need?' Small sounded worried. 'Finch can account for a lot of men.'

Webber did not share the other's doubts.

'Finch is past his best and he's used up his share of luck. I can handle him. You can leave him to me.'

Small looked at him closely.

'I'm mighty glad to hear that, Al,' he muttered. 'I never knew you was bullet-proof.'

'I can kill Finch in an open fight between the two of us but I'm not stupid enough for that. I cheat. I can't see any merit in giving a man a fair chance to kill me. I'll shoot him in the back or front or the roof of the mouth or the soles of his feet – any way I can get him.'

'I'm pleased that you've cleared up some of my doubts, Al,' growled Lindsay. 'For a minute there I thought you were planning a fair fight.'

Webber laughed. 'I might be tricky, but that's not one of my tricks.'

'It's a stand-off,' Cookson announced through the haze of cigar smoke in his office. The cigar box and the whiskey decanter had done the rounds of the assembled group but nobody had yet suggested a course that was legal and would still call Monson to account.

'We know those moonshiners were behind Harker's murder and that they were working for Monson,' Murchison added.

'That don't matter,' Durango said wearily. 'We've been over all this before. It's not worth a damn if we can't tie the moonshiners to Monson in a way that would stand up in a law court.'

Cookson turned to Parry.

'What do you think, young fella?'

'There's nothing I could say that hasn't already been said. Maybe if we wait a while something might come up. If Monson gives us the opportunity we might be able to clear out that rat's nest and claim self-defence, but he's hardly likely to do that.'

'Let's sleep on it,' Durango suggested. 'Someone might dream up a bright idea.'

Cookson's face showed he did not approve even though their planning seemed to have reached a dead end. Reluctantly he agreed.

'You're probably right, Durango. We'll call it a night – but I want to see everyone here at nine o'clock tomorrow morning.'

The group dispersed, doubtful that the new day would bring a solution to their problem.

It was mid-morning next day when they left the second conference in Cookson's office. This time the whiskey and cigars were noticeably absent. Heads were sorer and tempers shorter but no one had been able to offer any new ideas.

'I need a bit of the hair of the dog,' Durango complained. 'That whiskey of Cookson's slipped down pretty well last night. Maybe I got a bit too enthusiastic with it because I don't feel too sprightly this morning.'

'You won't find yourself too welcome in the saloon,' Parry told him. 'You would be about as popular as a rattlesnake at a Sunday school picnic.'

Murchison joined them and leaned against a veranda post while he filled his pipe.

'I don't think our sleep did us much good last night. I was feelin' fine when I went to bed. I should have stayed there for all the good this morning's meeting's done. We ain't any further along than we were last night.'

Parry looked casually along the town's single street. As he watched a buckboard came into view. He recognized it as the vehicle of the mail contractor who was making his weekly delivery and pick-up of mail from the general store, which also incorporated a post office. Tapping Durango on the arm, he pointed.

'Something's wrong. Looks like the team has bolted.'

SIXTEEN

Drawn by a pair of fiery little Spanish mules the buck-board shot past the general store and made straight for Cookson's depot. The watchers saw the driver shaking the reins and urging his team to maximum speed. Then, fifty yards short of the onlookers, he shouted 'Whoa!' At the same time he put his foot on the brake and hauled back on the reins. The locked wheels skidded and raised a cloud of dust as the well-trained mules sat back in their harness and brought the vehicle to a sliding stop.

Dick Conroy, the driver, was well known in Logjam Creek but he had never been considered a dangerous driver.

'Conroy, are you trying to kill someone?' Murchison called angrily as dust billowed around him.

'Joe! Look in the tray. There's a fella there lying on the mailbags. Wants to see you and Cookson real urgent.'

As the wagon master went closer a figure in the buckboard's tray sat up. His grey-streaked hair was long and untidy and a wild beard covered the lower part of his face. His shirt and trousers were ragged and dirty and dust partly obscured his features.

'Joe,' the apparition croaked, 'it's me – Ollie Harker.'

For an instant Murchison stood wide-eyed and open-mouthed; then he managed to speak.

'Ollie! Where have you been? We thought you were dead.'

'A couple of times I nearly was. I've been kidnapped, shot and nearly died, hunted by Indians, lost and starved. Never thought I'd see this place again.'

'I found him a few miles away sitting at the side of the trail,' the mail contractor told them. 'He was too weak to go any further.'

'Standing out here in the sun won't do him any good,' Durango suggested. 'Let's get him inside.'

As willing hands were helping Harker from the buckboard Cookson arrived. He edged past the helpers and put an arm around Harker's shoulders.

'We'd given you up for dead, Ollie. It's good to see we were wrong. You look like you've been under a buffalo stampede. Come inside and we will get you fed and watered and cleaned up. After that, when you feel better, you can tell us what happened.'

Having delivered his passenger the mail contractor turned his vehicle and drove to the post office, which was set up in the general store. He secured the buckboard and hauled in a large dusty mailbag destined for the Logjam Creek area. People who had seen him arrive knew that something was amiss and Conroy told them the little he knew.

One of the onlookers was an employee of Monson, who had come to collect the mail. Instead of doing so the man quietly left the group and hurried back to the saloon. This news was the last thing that Monson wanted to hear.

Webber knew something was amiss and he also headed for Monson's office. He could hear his boss swearing before he came through the door.

'What's happening?' the saloon owner asked.

'Ollie Harker's alive. Conroy just brought him to town.'

'That can't be . . . Crane and the others said he was given to the Indians. They reckoned that in that way nobody could claim that they had killed him. The whole thing was meant to look like he was grabbed by the Cheyennes. I should have known better than to trust those idiots.

'We're in real trouble now because Harker can probably tie us to his kidnapping, as well as to supplying liquor to the Indians.'

Webber thought for a while.

'I don't suppose we could silence Harker somehow. . . ?'

'It's too late for that,' Monson snarled. 'Cookson's no fool; he probably has Harker safely guarded. He might wait for the law or he might decide to settle things right now.'

'If we get in first and kill Harker and Cookson, saying they attacked us first, a good lawyer might still keep us out of trouble. If we can make them attack us here we might be able to trap them somehow.'

Monson saw a glimmer of hope.

'You could be right, Al. Get our men together and we can start planning this.'

Logjam Creek had no doctor but Cookson had employed a former military hospital steward to care for any injured workers until they could be removed to a doctor or nursed in the town until the doctor could be brought in from Hammondstown, fifty miles away. Harker had a bullet wound in his side, his feet were lacerated from walking in worn-out moccasins and he was starving.

Cookson had employed Jack Bassett, a former military hospital steward, who now took charge of the patient and ushered the others outside.

'This man needs rest and some food and maybe a small shot of whiskey. He's not fit to be talking too much at present. I'll get him cleaned up and put to bed. When he is a bit stronger I'll call you and he can tell his story.'

'How long will that be?' Cookson asked.

'Give him a couple of hours. At present he's completely exhausted – he could have a heart attack in this condition. I'll call you as soon as he is well enough to talk.'

Cookson turned to Murchison.

'Start getting our men together. I want only single men. Married men living here in town should remain at home because when the shooting starts we don't want Monson's crew taking shelter in nearby houses –

or maybe taking hostages. We have repeating rifles in the store room for anyone who doesn't have his own. Send the single men who are prepared to fight here as soon as they can get a gun. We don't know how long we have.'

SEVENTEEN

Webber watched the greatly increased activity around Cookson's office and tried to calculate the odds opposing him. He figured that his side would have fewer numbers but doubted that their enemies had the number of skilled gunmen that the Monson camp possessed. Himself, Keller, Lìndsay, and Small could give a good account of themselves; Monson, with a couple of hastily recruited saloon regulars, could provide a second line of defence if the saloon was attacked.

The main problem was that the building and its surrounds needed a fair number of men to guard its approaches. He wondered briefly if it would be better to seize the initiative rather than give the opposition time to plan their tactics.

He discussed the idea with Monson but the saloon owner was not in favour of opening the hostilities.

'Best we wait for them to attack. Then we can claim self-defence when the law comes around later. Somehow we need to trick the others into attacking first and so lure them into a trap.'

'We don't have the numbers for that,' Webber told him. 'We need to do them a lot of damage first and knock the fight out of them. Finch and maybe Parry are the most dangerous. We have to get them first.'

'That might not be as easy as it looks,' Small told him. 'With a gunhand like Finch it's dangerous to get your ambitions mixed up with your capabilities.'

Webber gave a grimace that sometimes served him for a smile. 'I'm getting an idea. How would you and Lindsay like to be the bait in a trap?'

'I have a worrying notion of who we're supposed to trap,' Small said nervously. 'It's Durango Finch, ain't it? Why the hell can't you be the bait?'

'Because I'll be waiting for him with a shotgun while you attract his attention and bring him into range. He has a bit of respect for me and might stand off a bit. He would be mighty careful with me but with a couple of noisy drunks he won't be so suspicious. I'll get him before he gets a shot at you two.'

'I wish I was as sure of that as you seem to be, Al. We'll talk it over while you figure out a safe plan. When we hear the plan we'll decide.'

Not far away Cookson and his employees were anxiously awaiting Harker's account of his experiences. Bit by bit the injured man gave details that explained his disappearance. He had been travelling alone when the moonshiners held him up and diverted his wagon to where their own was broken down with a collapsed wheel. They transferred their equipment and swapped wagon canopies in an effort to disguise the stolen vehicle. Harker was forced to drive to the hidden camp while one member of the gang carefully burned the old wagon to make it look like an Indian attack. He heard the name Monson mentioned and had little doubt that the saloon owner was running the operation.

When he enquired about his own fate he was told that word had been sent to the Indians that liquor trading was about to start. When the customers arrived he would be handed to them. If his mutilated remains should be found later the hostile warriors would be held responsible.

He was quickly robbed of all personal possessions, even his boots. Under guard he was also forced to help transfer the moonshine from a holding tank to bottles, which would allow the Indians to move away from the area if it looked as though they might be discovered.

During the bottling process the moonshiners had decided to sample their latest batch; it proved to be stronger than they'd expected; it was greatly in need of dilution. Harker told his listeners that when the powerful liquor started to take effect on his captors he'd seen a slight chance of escape.

One of the moonshiners had left to destroy the old wagon. When he returned, in his haste to sample the new whiskey he had left his saddled pony standing near by. Realizing this, Harker had run across the rough ground as fast as his bare feet would allow, then he had jumped on to the horse, which was standing ground-tied.

The moonshiners responded too slowly and the horse was almost out of pistol range when they loosed a volley of shots. One struck home breaking a rib before it exited on the other side of Harker's body.

'You were lucky, Ollie,' Cookson told him as he stood at the bedside.

'Didn't seem much like luck at the time. I was having trouble breathing and that horse just run away with me. I had no idea of where we were going and I knew that the Cheyennes would be in the area somewhere.

'I don't know what happened but somehow I fell off that mustang in a clump of trees. It was dark when I woke up. Every move I made hurt like hell and I wondered if the moonshiners or the Indians might be tracking me. I got up and forced myself to walk. I don't know how far I got before I passed out again.'

'How long were you unconscious?' Murchison asked.

Harker frowned and shook his head.

'I don't know, Joe. I'm mighty weak. Let me rest awhile and I'll tell you the rest later.'

'Sure,' said Cookson. He turned to the others. 'Everybody out. We can hear the rest when Ollie feels better.'

Monson was feeling more confident as the day wore on. No challenge came from Cookson's organization and he suspected a degree of hesitancy.

The allegations against him would only stand up to legal scrutiny if he could be connected with the dead moonshiners – and he was being very careful to remove all traces of their association. If the dispute with Cookson ended in gunfire he could always claim he'd acted in self-defence. Careful planning would be necessary but it was possible to both destroy his enemies and avoid falling foul of the law. Too much of Monson's money was tied up in Logjam Creek and the option of running never entered his mind.

He remembered the belongings that the moonshiners had taken from Ollie Harker. There was a wallet, a tobacco pouch and a couple of old personal letters, all now held in the large brown envelope in his desk drawer. Once they were gone he could think of nothing else that would connect him with the whiskey-runners.

He sealed the envelope and took it to where Webber and his men were playing pool, waiting for the shooting to start. He tossed it on to the table, thereby ruining Keller's shot.

'I want this taken outside and burned,' he ordered. 'Make sure it is completely destroyed.'

Parry was restless. He was sure that the bad blood that had been engendered would not be purged without gunplay. Cookson was trying too hard to stay within the law when there was no lawman for a hundred miles. Direct action would be needed if Monson's crew were to be brought to justice. Rather than waiting around he decided to spy out the saloon that was now the enemy's stronghold.

EIGHTEEN

The same brush-covered ridge ran behind both premises and Parry knew that he would be able to find a concealed vantage point from which to spy on Monson's defences. His one concern was that the saloon-keeper might have sent one of his henchmen on a similar errand. Cautiously he made his way along the side of the ridge, pausing occasionally to look and listen. Progress was slow but eventually he reached a spot that afforded a good view of the saloon. Lying concealed beneath a bush, he studied the scene below him, Almost immediately he saw three men around a small fire behind the building. He removed the small telescope from his hip pocket, opened it and trained it on the group. They were feeding papers into the fire.

He recognized Monson and Webber but not the third man, whose trade was indicated by a holstered gun positioned for a fast draw. They were deep in conversation and occasionally Monson would wave a hand in the direction of Cookson's depot, but they were too far away for him to hear what was being said.

Parry knew from the way the fire was being so carefully tended that the men were burning evidence. Cookson would not be happy that the only remaining proof of Monson's involvement would be Ollie Harker's testimony, which was far from conclusive.

For the next half-hour he studied the ground between the rival camps. They were on the same side of the road, about a hundred yards apart. The space between was open except for a couple of large corrals belonging to Cookson. As both buildings faced the street, only a couple of windows had views of the open space between. But the veranda in front of the saloon projected further towards the street and Monson stored empty barrels there, whence they could be more easily loaded into wagons and taken back to the suppliers. These barrels formed a screen that could conceal a couple of shooters, so Parry studied them carefully. Quickly he espied a couple of gaps and he mentally marked the spot as a possible defensive position.

One smaller barrel caught his eye. It appeared to have been arranged to create a loophole in the barrier. Most whiskey barrels were marked with the distillers' names in black paint but the smaller barrel appeared to have red writing. More out of curiosity than anything else Parry tried to read the brand. Because of the angle he could only read the letters TAB above a letter S. They meant nothing until he had closed the telescope and made his way back to the freight depot. As he walked into the office, he suddenly realized that he might have discovered something significant.

141

Murchison was sitting at a desk with his feet on it.

'Find anything useful?' he asked in a tone that scarcely concealed his pessimism.

'I found that we need to attack the saloon from the front or the back. There are a couple of second-storey windows facing us and he's built a wall of barrels on the saloon veranda. However we go at it, we have a lot of open ground to cross.'

'We might not be attacking anyone. J.B.'s not keen on starting a shooting war with no solid evidence.'

'I doubt there'll be much of that left. I saw Monson and a couple of others burning stuff behind the saloon. One thing though – that special beer that Cookson buys from Denver. Do they sell that at Monson's saloon?'

'No. Most beer goes off when it can't be carried by railroad. Monson usually only stocks whiskey. J.B. buys that special beer for himself because it stays good even when carried on ox wagons – something about how it's made.'

'Do you know how the barrels are branded?'

'I should. I've carried a few of them over the years. The keg's a small one, about nine gallons. It has Tabur's Special written on it in red paint – but what's this all about?'

'There's a keg like that stacked at the side of Monson's saloon. I got a good look at it from up on the hill. I couldn't read the full name but it looks like it's the one from Harker's wagon. The moonshiners must have sent it to Monson along with some of Harker's stuff. I think they've been burning evidence but forgot about that barrel.'

A smile spread across Murchison's face. 'Now we have that murdering sonofabitch. J.B. has the receipt for it and that weasel will have a hard time explaining how he got the barrel. See what else you can see – but don't go too far away because I reckon things are about to happen around here.'

'Any more news about Harker?' Parry asked.

'Yes. He told us he woke up inside a tepee. Scared hell out of him. But an old squaw man named Allard lived there. He and his Cheyenne wife found him unconscious and took him to their camp. He doesn't camp with his in-laws and they leave him alone.'

'I know Jackson Allard. He's a good man despite what some folks say about squaw men. What happened then?'

'They saved his life. The bullet had gone clean through Harker but Allard probed the wound while he was unconscious and cleared out a couple of shreds of his undershirt and shirt. If they had been left in, the wound could have gone bad and killed him. After that Ollie started improving – but Allard was taking a risk in hiding him.

'As soon as he was steady on his feet he gave his visitor a pair of moccasins his wife had made, a supply of buffalo jerky and rough directions on how to reach the wagon trail. He was to travel by night and hide by day. As you would imagine, travelling on dark nights meant that he sometimes went astray. A couple of times he saw small groups of Indians pass close to where he was hiding but luckily they didn't see him.

'He figured it took him weeks to really find where he was. By then the jerky had run out, the moccasins were falling to bits and Ollie was trying to live on berries. He was all but finished when Dick Conroy found him beside the trail.'

'What are his chances now?'

'Jack Bassett reckons he should get better as long as Monson's men can't get a shot at him.'

Later in the day, once the wagon boss had told Cookson about the discovery of the evidence, Parry met Murchison again and asked, 'What are we doing about that nest of skunks?'

Murchison looked about.

'J.B.'s thinking of hitting them tomorrow morning,' he said in a conspiratorial tone. 'He sent a man out to the ridge to check that barrel through a powerful spy-glass and he confirmed that it is the right one. Now that J.B. has solid evidence he is ready to act. He'll give us the details tonight.'

NINETEEN

The meeting that night in Cookson's office did not last long. As a former military officer in the Mexican war, Cookson had pored over improvised maps of the town and marked places where riflemen on both sides would have good fields of fire. He could afford only two men to cover his advance but both were armed with repeating rifles.

With these in position he would lead an attack with a force of eight men. Of these Durango would select three, whom he would lead around the back of the building and try to gain entry. J.B. would lead the remaining four men to flank the barrel wall and attack the front of the saloon. All employees who participated would receive a healthy bonus.

Parry would have preferred to go with Durango's group but his proficiency with firearms was needed to strengthen Cookson's group. The men would be in position before sunrise after a system of watches had been arranged for the night hours. It was doubtful, though, that anyone slept soundly. All were aware that a considerable element of luck would be needed if bloodshed was to be avoided.

By sunrise the group had eaten breakfast and were nervously checking their weapons as they waited for Cookson's orders. In stark contrast Durango stood aside, silently looking through a window at the deserted street. Parry walked over to him.

'You don't seem worried by what's about to happen,' he said. 'I suppose you're used to this.'

'I've never got used to this,' the gunman replied in a low voice, 'and, for your information, I'm scared stiff. The more of these situations I see the harder they are for me to face. Sure, I'll still take my chances and do what I'm paid to do, but I know that one day my luck will run out. In fact I have a strange feeling that today could be the day.'

Parry was momentarily lost for words.

'I'm not looking forward to this either,' he admitted eventually, 'but I'm hoping we can win. We all think we are lucky to have you on our side.'

'I hope that that confidence is not misplaced. If anything should happen to me I have left instructions for my planting with Cookson.'

Before Parry could comment further a couple of gunshots broke the morning calm and a raucous voice was heard yelling:

'Durango, you yellow coyote, come out and fight.'

Small and Lindsay had strolled unsteadily out into the street in front of the saloon, alternately swigging from and then brandishing whiskey bottles.

'Come out, Finch. We ain't scared of you. You don't have to hide from us if you're as good as people say.'

'Looks like Cookson's plans might have to be changed,' Durango said. He moved his holsters into more convenient positions. 'If I can knock that pair out of the fight the rest of Monson's crew might decide not to risk being killed.'

'It's a trap,' Parry warned. 'Don't fall for it. Where's Webber? He's more dangerous than that pair of drunks.'

'I know there's monkey business afoot. That pair are not even giving good imitations of drunks. I want you to cover me with a rifle. Shoot anyone who interferes with a gun of any kind.'

'Don't take the bait. There's sure to be someone backing up that pair. They're standing in front of the saloon; from this angle we can't get much of a look at what's there.'

The challenges were repeated and instinctively all eyes were turned on Durango.

'Don't meet them on the road,' Parry said urgently. 'Try to get them to move to the open ground between the two buildings. Our men can cover the only two windows on that side.'

Durango stepped out into the road.

'Move off the street,' he shouted. 'We don't want stray bullets hitting folks living near the saloon.'

Behind the wall of barrels Webber silently cursed. He had taken a shotgun into concealment with him, not expecting that Finch would make himself such a plain target for a rifle. He squirmed around in the confined space and with great difficulty found a gap that he could shoot through, between the barrels, but his intended target would need to come much closer.

Durango moved off the road on to the vacant ground between the buildings.

The two gunmen mirrored his move. Now they were openly nervous and Lindsay hastily glanced back over his shoulder as if to ensure that support was near by.

'You're a yella sonofabitch, Finch,' Small bellowed in a voice that no longer sounded quite so drunk. He knew that a couple more paces would bring Durango into range of Webber's shotgun.

Parry moved out into the street; he was certain that treachery was being planned but he could not see where Webber would be concealed. The wall of barrels was the most obvious place but at first he saw no sign of the threat that he suspected lurked there. Then the low early-morning sun glinted on metal and he could just discern a gun muzzle aimed at a point that Durango would cross in the next couple of strides.

He whipped the carbine to his shoulder and fired at the small amount of gun barrel that he could see, The barricade rocked as the bullet hit one of the metal keg hoops before bouncing off to bury itself in the wooden staves. Shocked by the near miss, Webber reeled back, dislodging other barrels in the process. Another closely placed Winchester slug from Parry set him in full retreat.

Small and Lindsay reacted differently. Small went for his gun but a shot from Durango knocked him down. Lindsay gave up all thoughts of fighting. Both his hands shot skywards.

'Don't shoot!' he screamed. 'For God's sake, don't shoot!'

'Drop your guns and get out of the way,' Durango called. Then, seeing that Lindsay was complying, he threw a couple of shots at the badly disarranged barrel wall.

All planning was forgotten in the sudden change of fortunes. Parry sprinted for the front of the saloon, throwing shots through any windows he saw.

The old warhorse came out in Cookson. Brandishing a rifle, he led his men forward.

'Come on, boys! Keep 'em running.' But his age caught up with him and he tripped and fell in the dusty street.

Murchison stopped, checked that his boss had not been injured, then helped him to his feet.

'I reckon we're both getting a mite old for this, J.B.,' he said.

'Pigs' eyelashes we are!' was the reply. 'Let's catch up with the boys.'

Maintaining the element of surprise, Parry and Durango burst through the front double doors together. A gun roared as a red muzzle flash flared from a dark corner of the barroom. The bullet hit no target but the flash pinpointed the shooter's position. Both men fired at once and a man fell across the table that previously had concealed him.

From halfway up a staircase another of Monson's gunmen fired at the Cookson crew, who were rushing through the open doors. A snap shot from Durango knocked his legs from under him and the man tumbled down the stairs. Foolishly, he retained his hold on his gun, and as he sat up Hockley shot him.

The barroom was now full of powder smoke. The shooting stopped momentarily, to be replaced by the sound of boots clattering on floors as men moved from room to room and bumped into or moved furniture.

The dusty figure of Cookson came through the door; he was partly supported by Murchison.

Without taking his gaze from the top of the stairs Durango backed across.

'There are too many of our people in here and someone could get shot,' he said. 'Best get a few outside to make sure nobody leaves the building. Tom and Hockley and I can make sure that no one upstairs gets down again.'

Murchison quickly passed the order to a group of late arrivals.

'Get back outside and cover the doors and windows,' he said. 'Shoot anyone who ain't a Cookson man if he tries to leave.' He turned to his boss. 'Best if we go too, J.B.. These boys know what they're doin'. No point in getting hit by stray lead.'

Cookson agreed with the idea but, in an effort to limit further bloodshed, he called out:

'This is J.B. Cookson. Anyone wants to surrender should throw down their guns and come out through the main bar with their hands up. I guarantee you will be safe as long as nobody tries any tricks. You have one minute to decide.'

150

Seconds later the door leading to the kitchen opened and, one after another, guns were kicked out and went skidding across the floorboards.

'Don't shoot,' a man called nervously. 'There's three of us. We surrender.'

The badly shaken trio were ushered out of the room by Murchison and placed under guard. When questioned they said that Webber and Monson were somewhere on the upper storey with an unknown number of men.

'Last chance,' Cookson called. 'Surrender now or it will be too late.'

From the floor above came a trampling of boots and the sound of a door opening. A wild-eyed man appeared at the top of the stairs with both hands in the air. Whatever he was trying to say was drowned out by the roar of a shotgun and he came tumbling down the stairs to join the other dead man at the foot of the bloody, uncarpeted steps.

Durango reloaded his guns.

'Looks like time to finish the job,' he said grimly to Parry and Hockley. 'Cover me as I go up those steps. Feel free to shoot anyone you happen to see before I do.'

Parry laid aside his carbine and drew his Colt. He knew that the fighting to come would be at close range and matters would be settled one way or another before he and Durango had emptied their revolvers.

Hockley stood back, his rifle at his shoulder aimed at the head of the stairs.

'I'll put a few shots through the walls at the top of

the stairs,' he said quietly. 'They are only made of soft pine; at this range rifle bullets will go straight through them. I might get someone lurking around a corner. I'll fire four shots. Count them. After that you will be in my line of fire.'

Durango cocked both six-shooters and nodded.

'I'm going first,' he told Parry. 'Good luck, *amigo*.'

Hockley opened fire; the rifle sounded like a cannon in the confined space.

Immediately after the fourth shot Durango and Parry reached the foot of the stairs but they were delayed slightly, having to step on and over the dead men before they found firmer footing.

Halfway to the top a bloodied Al Webber stepped clear to meet them. The sawn-off shotgun in his hands spat a lethal charge at the attackers.

It will never be known who fired first as all three men squeezed their triggers within a fraction of a second.

Parry saw the hat fly from Durango's head as the big gunman reeled against the wall, but he concentrated on Webber, swinging the unfired gun barrel in his direction.

Through the haze of powder smoke he triggered two quick shots. He saw Webber topple over, dropping the gun as he did so. With the most dangerous adversary out of the way, Parry bounded to the top of the stairs. He found Monson lying just round the corner. One of Hockley's shots had struck him in the side of the head when it tore through the dividing wall.

A quick check showed no other lurking enemies.

The noise from downstairs increased and a babble of voices told him that the fight was over. Then he had time to think about Durango.

TWENTY

It took several men to shift the dead and lift the fallen gunman off the stairs to place him on the bullet-pocked bar. Blood was flowing freely from a head wound. Parry pushed through the men clustered around.

'How is he?'

'I think he'll survive.' It was Cookson who answered. 'Looks like one pellet struck his fancy silver hatband and another ploughed a furrow across his head, but from what we can see it only cut the scalp and ruined his hat. Most of the slugs missed him. He's starting to come around. He might have a bit of a headache but he's probably had hangovers that were worse.'

'Anyone else of ours hurt?'

'Not a one,' Murchison said. 'Our plans were thrown out of kilter when you and Durango started things on your own, but it worked out for the best. I was expecting to see a few casualties on our side.'

The wounded gunman came around as Bassett was bandaging his head. He mumbled a few words, then lapsed into silence for a while. Eventually he asked in a faint voice:

'What about Monson?'

'He's dead,' Cookson said. 'Looks like Hockley got him with a lucky shot through a wall. I reckon you and Tom might have to share Webber's scalp between you. Both of you hit him with fatal shots.'

'I know I hit him dead centre,' Durango asserted. 'He was a dead man when he fired that shotgun. A man shooting downhill quickly always fires high. Webber knew that and might have got the pair of us if he hadn't already been dead on his feet. Tom was mighty helpful but Webber is my kill.'

Parry did not argue but secretly wondered how Durango could be so positive.

The week that followed was a busy one. Monson's surrendered men were given the task of burying their former comrades. When pressed to reveal details of their late boss's business deals, all professed ignorance. Though he was sure that they were lying Cookson recorded a few details about each, partly to satisfy future legal enquiries; then, to everyone's amazement, he set them free.

He paid each man thirty dollars out of Monson's money and gave them an old buckboard and a pair of mules that had belonged to their former employer. For self-protection on the trail they were given a shotgun and a single-shot rifle and each man was given an old revolver with five chambers loaded. Then, with dire warnings never to return, they were sent on their way.

'You were too easy on them, J.B.,' Murchison protested. 'That bunch of skunks will only cause trouble somewhere else. They should have been made to pay for their part in Monson's game.'

'They will be.' Cookson chuckled. 'Not half of them will get to wherever they plan to go. There's no loyalty among them and you can bet your boots that already they are scheming to get hold of the money they know the other thieving rats have.

'Before long they will start killing each other and the more ruthless among them will try to take everything. They won't ever know a moment's rest while they are together. The greedier ones won't let the others leave the group with money. Their final days will be mighty anxious times for all of them.'

'What does Harker think of the way things have panned out?'

'He's happy just to be among friends and getting back on his feet. There were times I misjudged him but he will always have a place in my organization. That reminds me, Tom. Now that the hunt for Harker is over I can find a job for you if you want one.'

'Thanks, Mr Cookson, but I am planning a new life. If you need a tracker or maybe a hunting guide I'll be happy to help out when I can, but now I will be working mostly for myself.'

Cookson laughed. 'You will find that you are the toughest boss you ever worked for, but good luck to you.'

With his work finished Parry took Kitty riding as often as they both had free time. They were happy, laughing, excursions as he showed her the interesting aspects of the country he knew so well.

Then he found himself counting the hours until their next meeting and lingering a little longer when the time came to part. Such a depth of feeling was new to him but Kitty showed none of the inner confusion he had been experiencing. She was always laughing, friendly and kind to everyone. He hoped she might find him something special but remained unsure.

A couple of times they visited George Roberts because an idea was forming in Parry's mind. After consulting his old friend he decided to file a homestead claim for a quarter section along the same permanent creek. As they explored along the stream, he explained his plans to Kitty.

'George and I are thinking of going into partnership. Between us we will have enough room to raise a few cattle that we can run on the open range when their numbers increase. As part of the homestead deal I must build a house. I was wondering if you would like to pick out a spot – just sort of from a woman's point of view.'

'Not all women might agree about the best place, Tom.'

'Your judgement will be fine for me, Kitty.' He spoke carefully as though a wrong word might cause a massive disaster. 'I sort of hoped you might even be interested in living here some day. But that's up to you. It seems that I have spent half my life hunting and tracking lost, stolen and strayed stock. Times are changing and the old days will soon be gone. It's time

I settled down and started a more permanent life.'

'You could always get steady work with Mr Cookson,' Kitty reminded him. 'I know he thinks highly of you.'

Parry shook his head. 'Although I've often done the odd job for J.B. I will never be known as a Cookson man. I am my own man and I will succeed – or maybe even fail – by my own efforts. I can't offer much but I'm wondering if you might throw in with me?'

Kitty smiled. 'Tom Parry, are you proposing marriage?'

'I guess I am. What do you think?'

She ranged her pony beside his horse, stood in her stirrups and planted a passionate kiss on his lips.

'That sounds like a good idea to me.'

The sun had barely risen when Parry met Durango outside the bunkhouse in Logjam Creek. Durango had changed greatly. The expensive black hat was gone and he wore a cheaper grey Stetson. One revolver was tucked away in the large bedroll behind his saddle and his boots were now looking worn and dusty. A grey-flecked beard was sprouting; already he looked older.

Standing by Midnight's head, he spoke quietly to Parry.

'Time I was gone, *compadre*,' he said. 'You know, I might even miss some folks around here. You're as good a man as I have ever seen and it was nice knowing you. I don't mind telling you that because we won't meet again.'

'You never know; we might meet up again some-where.'

'I doubt it. Durango Finch will be dead as soon as I am clear of this part of the world. I'm sick of this life and I am going to change my name and head for a city somewhere where folks have never heard of me. I have saved a bit of money and I hope to buy into a nice quiet little business, something boring and peaceful where I never need to carry a gun again.

'An editor over in Kansas owes me a big favour and when my tracks are suitably covered, he will publish a short piece saying that I have died peacefully of an accident or natural causes. The word will eventually filter through the West. You will read it and, as a friend, I will ask you to agree with the report if people ask. Will you do that?'

'I sure will. But one thing has always puzzled me. Why are you so sure that it was your bullet that killed Al Webber? You never struck me as a man who kept score, like some sort of scalp-hunter.'

'I knew you would be wondering. I suspected too that you would be curious and maybe even a little disappointed in me, but I was doing you a favour. Webber was acquiring a name as a gunslinger and if you became known as his killer some of his friends or even some other would-be gunslinger might be anxious to see just how good you are. I don't know whose bullet killed him but it's best if his name goes on the record as the deceased Durango Finch.'

'I'm glad you told me that. Here's my hand on it. I'll keep your secret.'

Durango shook his hand and stepped into the stirrup.

'Good luck to you and Kitty.'

Resisting a sudden feeling of solemnity, Parry made a joke.

'Of course I won't miss you bitching about the hard ground and cold nights we shared together. We were a fairly mismatched team.'

'But we worked well together.' Durango laughed. As he wheeled the black horse about and cantered away he called over his shoulder:

'Good luck, *compadre*.'

The sun was higher and Parry wasted no time looking after the departing rider. He reckoned it was time to call in at the Pages' house, where he had a standing invitation to breakfast.